Special to
Richard + Sylvia [illegible]

Traitor

A Story of Irish Freedom

A J S Crawford

Cover design by Keith Crawford

Edited by Paul Vincent - www.doctoredit.co.nz

Web site and book format by Keith Shackleton - www.clikka.co.nz

Visit the web site at www.traitorthebook.com

First Edition: April 2013

ISBN 978-0-473-23869-8

Foreword

For some thirty-five years my family and I have been taking our summer break in Castletownshend, a few miles from Skibbereen in County Cork.

The beauty of the West Cork scenery and the generous welcome of its people have drawn us back yearly, and my brother, after a visit to us there, has purchased a summer house in the village and is a regular visitor three times a year.

His family and mine have roamed that area for three decades and indeed are as well known there as in my home town of Dungannon, County Tyrone. One day we came across the Kilmichael monument with the plan of the ambush and related tombstones, at which point he, my brother, challenged me to write a story from the Republican point of view, knowing that I was a Northern Protestant and a loyal British subject of the Queen, with a grandfather who had been a Sergeant in the Royal Irish Constabulary and a father who had served in both the RIC and then the Royal Ulster Constabulary, right through those troubled times.

I accepted the challenge and began to research the contemporary events and places and when I visited the site of James Connelly's burnt-out home, the story started to take shape in my head.

I was a Primary School Headmaster and sadly had lost my sight. Fortunately, about that time I was lucky enough to have a children's script accepted by a lady called Bernagh Brims, Chief Education Officer for the BBC Schools Programmes, thus beginning a lifetime's friendship and a writing career for her programmes, and much more.

This, then, is the fictional result of my wonderful holidays in Munster and, of course, my brother's challenge.

Prologue

In the *Concise Oxford English Dictionary*, between 'trait' and 'trajectory', one finds:

> traitor, *n*. One who violates his allegiance or acts disloyally [to country, king, cause, religion, principles, himself, etc.]

Would I have the audacity to criticise such an august publication? This is a rhetorical question, for anyone who knew my father and anyone who knows me will understand that even in the most prodigious of texts, misprints and inadequacies may occur – which those two were only too ready to point out.

You see, some years ago now, I happened to have circumstances, as opposed to greatness, thrust upon me to the effect that there are for me many and varied interpretations of the word 'traitor'. And when it comes to traitors, Ireland has had more than its fair share.

Well, rather than ramble on, allow me to elucidate thus:

One

He was in his early forties, a man who might have been termed ruggedly handsome, but tonight the old anger and resentment smouldering in the narrowed eyes distorted his features as he watched from the upstairs window. Below their silhouettes were dark against the moonlight as they leaned together staring down over the rooftops stepped steeply down the main street of the little village to the flat calm of the long estuary.

'One more run, Mary,' whispered the young man as he kissed the top of her head. 'One last run an' that's a promise.'

She didn't answer for she had heard it all before, and yet, each time they needed him, his youthful adventurous spirit made him ready to go. She stared below where yellow oil lamps in the windows of the cottages lighted the unmetalled street down past the four trees in the middle of the way, to the harbour with its slipway and small quay. She wondered which of them it was.

'But Brendon,' she pleaded, her shoulders rising and falling in a great sigh of despair, 'they know now that the carrier is from this district. Someone has informed. They would surely have had you that last time if it hadn't been for the danger signal light flashin' on Toe Head. Somebody was surely lookin' after ye that night.'

'True for ye, my lovely,' he answered, running a finger down her cheek. 'I've often wondered who that Good Samaritan was.'

He was silent as the events of that run came back to him. He had been still a mile out at sea when, alert as a cat stalking a mouse, he had noticed the winking lamp high on the headland above the rocky inlet, and as he watched it kept blinking into some sort of pattern. He didn't understand but a nod was as good as a wink and he had ported his helm, picked up the off-shore breeze and sped away along that rugged coast to find the alternative drop beyond Tra Gumna. In the morning he had found out that they had been there all right. He would have sailed straight into their gentle arms and that most certainly would have been the end of all their dreams.

He shook himself.

'Probably some sympathetic farmer noticed them settlin' in for an ambush an' my boat approachin'. It wouldn't be hard to put two an' two together.'

'God bless him anyway, whoever he was,' said Mary, and nuzzled her head against his shoulder. 'You've done your share aye and more than your share an' you can't count on luck like that again. Surely there's someone else? Another place? Somewhere that hasn't a snake livin' among its people. God, Brendon there has to be someone else. You're not the only one with a sea-goin' boat and the skills to sail her.'

'No, but I'm the recent blow-in,' he answered. 'I'm the one who has none of the local baggage. I'm the innocent!'

'But they, the informer I mean, knows all about you,' she cried, exasperated.

'Aye girlie,' he answered, 'the rat knows as you say, but obviously he hasn't passed it on yet, my name I mean. There's a pile o' men with good boats but they're already bein' watched and there's a pile o' coves and inlets up and down the coast from Kinsale to Bantry. They'll need exact information an' the bastard hasn't yet got enough King's shillin's to tell them that. No, Mary, they'll never get me. They've asked me to do one more run, my love! Just one last night and then we'll head for me aunt's brother in Macroom as we've planned these three months past and leave it to them and him.'

He nodded towards the house and the watcher eased his face back into the deep shadow. The lad tightened his arm around her slim waist as he kissed her ear.

'Trust me, Mary! Trust me! I know what I'm doin'. The boys'll not let me down but God help the piece of dog-shit when they find him, that's all I say. They have their own way of dealin' with informers.'

Gently he turned her to face him and this time the kiss was warm and tender on her lips, before he eased her away to arm's length and looked for one long moment deep into her eyes, green in the moonlight that glistened on the tears, welling up in them. He started down the track. She watched his back till he raised an arm in salute without looking round and disappeared beyond the sharp bend in the road. Then she turned and slowly made her way across the stubbled grass to the old Coastguard house, dark-windowed and silent as the lonely mountain behind it.

In the chill of the night the watcher gently closed the crack in the heavy curtain and stood there for some moments deep in thought before crossing the room and crawling back into the high four-poster bed and pulling the blankets over his head.

Inside the kitchen Mary lit the lamp, stirred the turf into life, and sat down in her father's large armchair, resting her head back as the tears wet her cheeks. In time the snoring from his room upstairs sawed her to sleep.

When she woke, stiff and cold, the grey dawn was paling the quartered window and she struggled up to throw turf on the hot ashes. Unhooking the leather bellows from the jamb, she soon had it blazing and swung the big heavy kettle on its crane over the flames. In no time she was sipping hot, sweet tea from her blue enamel mug. Refreshed, she placed the big iron pan on the glowing peat, cracking eggs into it along with slices of bacon from the fletch hanging from a smoky rafter by the chimney breast.

Soon the mouth-watering smell of an Irish breakfast was wafting through the entire building. Almost like a received signal, she heard his bedroom door open and his steps on the creaking stairs. He came into the kitchen, black-stubbled and dressed in collarless shirt under red braces holding up heavy dark trousers, and without a word sat down at the scrubbed table. His daughter set the plate in front of him and turned back to the fire to get her own.

'An' the top of the mornin' to you too, father,' she said. 'I trust you slept well.'

'How cud a body sleep wi' him about the place? Aye an' God knows what yis bees up te. Huh! If me an' the lads didn't need him, I'd soon give him short shrift, him an' his Northern uppity airs. There's somethin' about that boyo I don't trust for all his sugary talk,' he answered through a mouthful of sausage. 'Is there no fried soda?'

She flicked it off the pan and pushed across the plate.

'Well, dear father,' she said, sitting down opposite him, resting her elbows on the table and cupping her tea in her hands, 'you won't have to be bothered about Brendon for much longer for we're off next week and then you can fight with yourself, aye, and get your own fried soda bread. You're still a young man and perfectly able to do it. His aunt will see to ye as well. Ye always had a notion o' her anyway, ever since mother died. Oh I've watched the pair of yis. Well now's your chance if ye can spare the time from the other goin's on ye do be organisin', and of course prise her away from the bold Mr Heggerty. Wi' Brendon an' me out of the way, there's nothin' to stop ye.'

'You watch yer tongue on that score me girl,' he snapped, pointing the fork at her. 'My position'll not save ye if ye talk loose. None o' that's any o' your affair. Mind that well an' I'll thank ye to leave my private life to me as well. You keep your nose out of things that don't concern ye, me lass.'

'Och do ye think I don't know how yis reward traitors. Give me credit for some wit,' she retorted.

'Huh,' he grunted and resumed his meal.

'Well did ye hear what I said?' the girl went on. 'Brendon and me are leavin' next week. His grandfather in Donegal has left him money an' the wee farm o' land. He's sellin' the *Northern Star* an' with the proceeds we're for Macroom and his Uncle Harry's till the date for the Cork Ferry. Oh we've it all planned. There's a packet-steamer from there to Derry once a month an' we'll be on it before the end of October. There's nothin' for us here any more. He's finished an' so am I. We want our own life an' we're off an' nobody's goin' to stand in our way this time.'

He had stopped eating again during this final speech. Then in silence he finished his breakfast, drained his teacup and rose from the table. In the small back pantry he shaved and washed, before going back upstairs to get dressed. She was still sipping tea when he took his cap and stick from the back of the door and left without another word. Mary smiled at the departing back.

'That has given ye somethin' to think about, eh?' she said softly as she drained her mug and began gathering up the dirty dishes.

Two

Brendon wasn't due until the morrow though he was never far from her mind, imagining all that could go wrong on this last mission. He had promised it would be just that but well she knew that they didn't let you go so easily, never mind the present dangers. All day she went about her chores of feeding chickens, collecting and scouring eggs, milking the cow and washing and hanging out the clothes – more like an automaton than her happy laughing self. As the light faded and night drew down she climbed the stairs to bed and tossed fitfully through the hours of darkness, knowing he was out there somewhere risking his life for a cause she barely believed in, while her father snored loudly in the next room. She had heard him return around one from setting the night nets, and heard the bottle clinking on the glass when he took his nightcap as was his wont, before going up to bed.

The first glimmer of dawn roused her to another day of worry which increased as the hours dragged by and there was no sign of him. She knew Brendon would have his lobster pots to lift and re-bait but that would have been done before midday. The afternoon dragged by but still there was neither sight nor word. Her father was out with his partner, Michaeleen, checking his nets, and when he did return he informed her curtly that he had heard nothing.

It was too late! Something must have happened. For the umpteenth time she went to the window, peering out into the pale light of the hunter's moon but no other darkened figure had trudged up the path since that of her father who, after his supper and whiskey, had gone straight to bed. Far below, the sea was like a silver duck pond with scarcely a ripple and she could see Horse Island a low dark line, barely a mile from the mouth of the inlet. She never knew the details but she knew that out there somewhere was the rendezvous where the foreign ship would lie.

The hours dragged by. She could neither read nor rest. Something must surely have happened. He had been betrayed once more. The Tans had him and even now were employing their well-known gentle persuasions to extract information. Oh God, the very thought!

Suddenly there was a quick tapping at the back window. She sped to the kitchen door and the next moment she and the young man were wrapped in each other's arms.

'Oh Brendon,' she whispered, momentarily tilting her head to indicate the room above. 'Oh sweetheart, I thought they had got you. What happened? Are they after you? Why the mountain path?'

He put his lips on hers and then led her outside. He threw down his oilskin and together they sat down in the soft heather away from the house.

'They damn nearly did for me this time, Mary. Only I am the strong swimmer.' He paused to hold her again.

'What happened? This is the last isn't it? Oh Brendon!'

'They were waitin',' he went on. 'Knew the very spot. Thon wee pier at Castlehaven. They were hidin' in the graveyard. Jeeze it was close. They got the boat and the stuff but I rolled over the gunwale when some one of the eejits rattled a rifle bolt, just as I rounded the point. I'll bet ye he gets a ballockin' for his pains whoever he was, God bless him.

'Made it round to Sandy Cove and climbed up to Carey's. Michaeleen was still up, after settin' the night lines with yer father. He gave me dry clothes an' a few hot whiskeys. I've been there all day, waitin' for dark to come to you. It's a good thing I know the sheep tracks for I heard them on the road. When Michaeleen came back he made me wait till now for he passed two patrols on his way home. We kept tryin' to figure out who is the informer. On an' off all day we went over who it might be. I think he has his own idea but he wouldn't say. "We'll not put the black on any man till we're sure, Brendon," he said. "It would be a terrible thing to get wrong."'

He paused to draw breath and kiss her again as she clung to him, herself breathless with her anxiety.

'Then I came on to get here before daylight.'

He looked across at the lightening Eastern sky to his left.

'I daren't go home in case the informer gave me name an' they're watchin' at the cottage.'

'Oh thank God, thank the Holy Mother!' breathed the girl. 'You're safe. That's all that matters and we'll be off to Macroom next week. I've told him already.'

'Aye Mary my love but the Sergeant knows my boat, even if the rat didn't give me name. Every patrol between here an' Cork'll be on the lookout for me.'

They held each other in silence, the full horror of that situation sinking in. Then Mary eased him away from her and said excitedly, 'Surely 'tis true but couldn't you say it was stolen or borrowed without you knowin'? Yes it was stolen. That's the answer.'

Then, warming to her solution, she went on. 'They couldn't prove it wasn't so. Don't you see, Brendon? If you run you're guilty. If you face them, what can they prove? Nothin' but that someone took your boat without you knowin'. You were here all night with me. That has to be the answer, sweetheart.'

She was right. In fact they were both right. The Black and Tans were taking the cottage apart when he got down to the village just as the sun was coppering the long inlet. His aunt stood outside sobbing softly, a neighbour's arm around her while the Sergeant did his best to restrain the excesses of the pseudo-military personnel.

'Ah the prodigal returns,' said the young Lieutenant, slowly taking his revolver from the holster. 'And where have you been, pretty boy? Midnight stroll or just out for a sail in that fine green and white boat of yours? A strange catch, what?'

'If it's any of yer business,' replied Brendon, looking the man straight in the eye, 'I was with my fiancée all night.'

The soldiers grinned knowingly at each other, sniggered and made ribald remarks.

'There,' said his aunt, staring hard at the officer. 'Didn't I tell you? He went up to keep Mary company while her father was out on the night lines. I told you.'

'Aye,' said the Police Sergeant accompanying them, 'He's marryin' Mary McCarthy, the daughter. Lives up in the old Coastguard station. Her father Mick fishes. Aye that is the truth of it all right, Lieutenant Brown. They've been courtin' these twelve months past.'

He turned to Brendon.

'Who did ye lend yer boat to last night?' he asked pointedly, taking out his notebook.

'My boat?' echoed the youth. 'Nobody. I wouldn't lend the *Northern Star* to Pontius the Pilot himself. No way, Sergeant. Nobody gets my boat save I'm at the tiller. No bloody way!'

'So you have no idea how it got into Castlehaven Bay last night with a cargo of bags of chemical fertiliser?'

'Fertiliser?' echoed the youth, innocence personified. 'What are ye talkin' about Sergeant O'Reilly? I know nothin' about fertiliser an' anyway what's the harm in fertiliser? Can we not even grow spuds any more? Is it back to the famine ye want to drive us? Whoever had my boat has a damn cheek on them an' I'll bloody well find out who it was and believe me I won't be comin' to you when I do.'

'This'll take more investigation,' answered the Policeman, replacing the notebook in his breast pocket, slowly buttoning down the flap. 'I'll be havin' a word wi' Mary right this mornin' before you get to her an' ye'd better be tellin' me the truth.'

The Lieutenant listened grim-faced, and for a long minute stared at Brendon but the lad never flinched. Then he said slowly and deliberately, 'And now, Lieutenant, I would appreciate it if you'd get your bunch of thugs out of my aunt's house and take your business away from harassing helpless women. Or is that all you English are fit for? Damn pity the Germans couldn't put manners on yis.'

Everything stopped and the soldiers stood looking at their officer with only the raucous cacophony of the crows in the tall beech trees of the Castle grounds to disturb the ominous silence. For a moment anything could have happened. Villagers stared. His aunt put a hand to her mouth and the Lieutenant, himself scarcely a couple of years out of the mud, blood and guts of the trenches, eyes blazing, slowly raised the Smith and Wesson on its lanyard. Suddenly the Police Sergeant stepped between them, raised his fist and smashed Brendon hard across the face, drawing blood from his lip.

‘Watch yer tongue, ye Northern trash. Easy seen yer not a Cork man. We show a bit o’ respect when we’re talkin’ to the Law down here. Now get inside an’ mind I’ll be keepin’ a tight watch on ye from now on till I know a damn sight more about this night.’ His face was close to Brendon’s, one eye flickered imperceptibly willing silence.

Without a word, the youth strode into the cottage, followed by his aunt. For long moments it was still touch and go but at last the Policeman, arms spread wide like one shooing chickens in the backyard, broke the tension, ushering the onlookers away to their own affairs.

‘Come on now. No more to see here. Have you nothin’ better to do?’

Replacing the weapon in its brown holster and buttoning down the safety strap, the Lieutenant nodded at his Sergeant who barked an order and with a clattering of boots and rifles, the Tans piled into the high Crossley Tender which roared away up the steep street, back to the commandeered Masonic Hall in Skibbereen. The Policeman stared thoughtfully after it while wiping sweat from the inside band of his tall helmet with his handkerchief, before replacing it in the sleeve of his tunic. He looked towards the cottage where neighbours were helping to straighten the furniture. Then, shaking his head and with his hands behind his back, he turned down to his station residence, a troubled man, torn between two loyalties.

Three

The kitchen at the back of Heggerty's Bar was dimly illuminated. A heavy curtain had been drawn over the single window. The only light was the blazing of the turf in the open fire, glinting on the five pint glasses of stout on the table and shadowing the eyes in the five faces behind them.

'It was all too damned easy,' said the man at the head of the board. 'All too damned easy! They daren't lift him. They need him again. I tell yis it was too damned easy. Puttin' on a show, they were. A bloody show for the village. No notion o' liftin' him!'

'Ah feck it, Mick,' said Michaeleen, an open-faced, well-built fisherman in his mid-thirties. 'It couldn't be Brendon. Sure wasn't it meshelf that he came to, drownded like a rat. We talked some that night an' I'd swear by him. Oh I know he's a Donegal man wi' ideas above his station but he's a good lad for all that. Naw, Mick, I can't see it bein' Brendon.'

'I'm wi' you, Michaeleen,' said Heggerty, ten years the other's senior and just about showing a small increase around the waist. 'The lad's not the informer or I'm no judge. He bums a bit but what lad doesn't?'

'Aye an' his aunt's a fine-looking woman for her thirty-odd years, Seamus, what?' remarked a man in tweed jacket with leather patches on the elbows.

There was a general chuckle in the room.

'That has nothin' to do with it, Mr Murphy,' snapped the publican. 'I still know my duty.'

'That'll do,' said Mick, tapping the bottom of his glass on the wood. 'Keep to the business in hand. This scum has to be caught and dealt with, an' that damned quick. We don't know the ins and outs of the Macroom operation an' it's better we stay ignorant for the present, but I tell ye, we need another delivery an' that before All Souls Day or no more than a week after – an' this time it's not fertiliser. Now put yer minds to it. What man from around here could betray his comrades an' his country at the same time for the English shillin'?'

'Aye,' replied Murphy, tilting his head and letting his gaze rest on the others in turn. 'What man would do such a heinous deed?' He paused, thoughtfully rubbing his chin, then added, 'Or woman?'

There was a silence in the room.

'Hmmm,' said the fifth man, a small rat-faced bald character, staring into his pint.

'Now that's a thought worth considerin' so it is, Master. A woman, eh? We hadn't thought o' that possibility. Ye see what education does for ye, lads?'

'Ah don't be talking' like a horse's ass O'Boyle,' said Heggerty. 'Sure what woman would know the times an' places? Talk sense man.'

All eyes turned on the publican but only Mick spoke from the head of the table, for none but the Commandant dared.

'Any chance ye talk in yer sleep, Seamus?' he asked quietly.

'I'm not takin' this,' shouted the publican, knocking back his chair and leaping to his feet. 'I don't have to take that in me own house.'

'Sit down, Seamus,' said Mick. 'Sit down, man. I'm not getting' at ye and anyhow, yer both unattached adults. What ye do in yer own time is yer own business. As yer Commandant, I'm askin' a straight question. Is there any chance ye might talk in yer sleep?'

'How the hell would I know,' retorted Heggerty, resuming his seat with an ill grace. 'There is one thing I'm sure of no matter a damn if there's anythin' in what ye say. Annie is one of us through an' through. She's no informer. D'ye think she'd put her own flesh an' blood in danger? Let's all talk some feckin sense, not like a wasp lookin' for somewhere to light!'

'Hmmm,' said Mick, sipping his pint. 'That would be my thinkin' too about the lady but it doesn't alter my opinion of that nephew of hers. He knows the times an' places.'

'Of course, so do we all,' offered the schoolteacher quietly. 'So do we all,' and again he studied the faces around him.

Mary's father took out his pipe and proceeded to fill it from his pouch, slowly and methodically cutting the dark plug, snapping the penknife blade closed with a click and massaging the slivers in his hard hands. His companions sipped at their drinks. The room was silent, each deep in thought, figuring the pros and cons, jealousies and dislikes, long-past wrongs and distrusts, till Mick's pipe glowed red in the gloom.

'A trap,' he said at last. 'Put yer minds to it comrades. It's the only way. A trap for a rat!'

'Aye,' answered Michaeleen, 'but we haven't decided the bait. Who's the bait?'

'I have,' retorted Mick without hesitation. 'Even though he thinks he's marryin' my Mary, we have most reason to suspect him so he's the first. If necessary we'll go through others but he's the first. Remember, he's the only one hasn't taken the oath. That's my decision. Now let's get down to a plan for the Tipperary operation has a window in November is all I'm told an' there's no time to waste. Let me hear your suggestions.' And once more the room fell into thoughtful silence and supping.

Four

It was a few nights later, after a quiet but obviously animated conversation over the bar between Heggerty and Brendon, as the other four customers judiciously applied themselves to their card game in the far corner by the fire.

'Five draw,' said the small man in the green hat sporting the red cock-pheasant's feather. 'Tanners in,' and he began dealing, head slightly cocked to one side, like a listening bird.

Brendon drained his tankard and with a scowl, gathered up his jacket.

'Where to?' he hissed.

'Ye'll be met at the wee pier down the lane below Galley Head. Ye know it?' said the publican in a voice just audible to the lad. 'I know we've sprung it on ye but we want no leaks this time. It's tonight. There's no time for waggin' tongues. Be as near three o'clock as ye can. Ye'll be met. Same password. Positively the last run, Brendon. Good luck. Yeah, yeah, I know we promised but that other one doesn't count. This'll do it. Orders from higher up. Then you're off the books so to speak.'

'An' ye'd bloody well better believe it, Mr Heggerty. You'd better believe it. God knows what Mary'll say. I promised her the last time would be just that, the last run.'

The publican reached across his counter and grabbed the lad's forearm, resting there.

'You can't tell her,' he snapped. 'Not a word till it's over. That's an order from the very top. Not a single word!'

'An' here's an order for you, Mr Heggerty,' Brendon hissed, eyes blazing with anger. 'You tell them I'm finished. Done. Out. This is the very last run and be damned to them.' He pushed between empty tables and slammed down the steps into the street, bending his head against the rain as he made his way home.

As the pub door closed behind him, Michaeleen rose from the table.

'Deal me out this hand, Monaghan,' he said and, taking his glass, eased up to the bar.

'I'll try another, Seamus,' he said and lowering his voice added, 'Is the cheese in the trap?'

'It is, but not quite the way our leader thinks, God save us,' replied the publican moving the pump handle away and back, filling the pint tankard. 'There's just the five Army Council now who know where the real collection point is. Mick's conveniently away in Cork City on some errand or other, the Master's sound as a bell an' Baldy's on duty. If the lad's guilty, he has only a couple of hours at most to contact anyone and with O'Boyle watchin' him we'll know if he does.'

'Aye that wee shite'll not miss much. That's all he's good for. It wouldn't surprise me at all if he was the informer himself, always ready wi' the smart cracks,' answered Michaeleen, sipping thoughtfully at the creamy froth. 'Aye Brendon's the bait, but the trap is ours, Seamus, an' we have a fir notion who it'll catch. A fair idea!'

'I told him Galley Head, so as I say, only us five know the other.'

Michaeleen took out his pipe and busied himself with contemplation and tobacco plug.

'Hmm,' he said. 'So, if he's the one, the Tans should be at Spanish Head. I have detailed a Clon Volunteer to watch there to see if they turn up.'

'That's it, Michaeleen,' said Heggerty, 'an' if they're not there but at the real rendezvous, then the lad's in the clear an' we know for certain who's been at the sugar sack.'

'True for ye, Seamus,' returned his friend, putting a match to the tobacco and with a few practised puffs, and a hardened forefinger, had it well alight before continuing. 'Hmm. Just so. Just so, but we'll have to get our bit done first. Can't have the lad taken if he's innocent. Can ye close sharp?'

'No problem,' answered the publican. 'There's only the four o' them at the cards and but for Monaghan they have to rise for work in the mornin' so they'll not be late mid-week.'

'Right then,' said Michaeleen, 'see you round on the West Quay shortly after midnight. That should give us plenty of time. I have the other boxes already in my shmall boat. We should make it in an hour. OK?'

'See you then.'

He drained his tankard and made for the door.

'Goodnight lads,' he said, and waving to the card players he stepped down into the street, clicking the latch behind him and started up the hill and off along the Castlehaven Road.

Five

Brendon sat slumped in the big leather chair staring into the fire. From time to time he glanced at the clock on the mantelpiece.

'What is Mary going to say? I promised her faithfully and all the arrangements have been made. We're stayin' with your brother, Uncle Harry in Macroom for a few weeks while I get tickets an' that, aye an' decide where we're goin' finally. I've done my share. We were to get the train from Skibbereen tomorrow.'

'Where is it to be?' asked his aunt quietly, sitting across from him with some knitting or other.

'You know I can't tell you that, Aunt,' he answered, looking out at the inky night.

'Doesn't matter,' she answered casually. 'Just wonderin' how far and if ye'd be back in time. You know, how long would you be and maybe ye wouldn't have to alter your plans.'

He shrugged.

'I can't depend on that,' he answered and took another look out the kitchen window.

A thick mist was starting to roll up the estuary. At least that would be a help.

'I'm to be at the rendezvous about three,' he said, 'but the way things are, I can't guarantee what time I'll be back. I may have to run for it at best or—'

He didn't finish his sentence but he didn't have to.

His aunt looked across at him.

'Well you'd better go this last time,' she said. 'Scribble a note to Mary and I'll leave it up after you've gone.'

She rose, went into her bedroom to get her coat and run a comb through her fair hair in front of the mirror over the fireplace. She stared at herself, indecision in her hazel eyes. Then, picking up a lipstick, she touched her lips and moved them against each other to spread the colour evenly before dabbing scent behind each ear.

Quickly he scribbled some words on a torn sheet of jotter to inform Mary of the change in plans, stuck the envelope and left it on the table.

'Right,' he called to his aunt and glanced at the clock on the mantelpiece again: a quarter past twelve. Mary would be sound asleep by now, probably dreaming of their flight on the morrow. His uncle would not know of the change. Just too bad but they could easily borrow a trap in Bandon and a couple of hours would take them through Dunmanway and into Macroom. Then from there, who knew? Even America! Well the hell with it. He could still do it but Mary would have to make her own way to the station and board the train no matter if he was there or not. He would catch it somehow. He would not return no matter how things went, for after the last time he was not willing to risk being subjected once more to the gentle ministrations of the Black and Tans if the informer was at his dirty work and another escape had to be undertaken. God but he would have to keep his wits about him this night.

Hastily stuffing his few belongings into his rucksack with Annie's help, he took his oilskins from the back of the door.

'Be in touch, Aunt Annie,' he said. 'Get what ye can for the boat an' send it on. I'll let ye know the address. Tell Mr Heggerty he'll find her moored at Clonakilty or somewhere nearby.'

His aunt glanced sideways at him but said nothing.

'I'll try to catch the train there,' he told her taking a last look around his room.

He kissed her on the cheek and she held him tight for a moment.

'I'll see to it and I'm glad you and Mary are getting' out of here,' she said. 'Things are goin' to get worse before they're better. God bless the pair of you. Let me know where you finally decide to live. Take care, Sweetheart.'

He kissed her again and, struggling into his waterproof jacket, slung his bag over his shoulder and stepped out into the thin mizzle and headed down to the little harbour, totally unaware of the small dark figure deep in the shadow of the entry opposite. Allowing him some fifty yards start, it emerged and, keeping close to the wall, started silently after him but froze in his stride as the quiet voice from across the street whispered, 'Mr O'Boyle, a moment if you please,' and he could just make out Annie, silhouetted by the oil lamp behind, standing at her front door.

'How's your wife?' she asked softly. 'The baby should soon be arriving, eh? Oh and how's Maureen, that pretty servant girl. Still willing?'

Brendon untied the *Northern Star* and, with the oars, eased her slowly from the wall and out into the ebbing tide, little knowing that away up the hill in the old Coastguard house, Mary slept soundly and did not hear the creak of the stairs as her father went down into the hall in response to a pebble on his window and opened the heavy door to the note-bearer.

'Ah you're back,' she said softly. 'I wasn't sure when I saw no light.'

'Oh I'm back an hour or more,' he whispered. 'The last train. Had to walk the whole cut out. Just been sittin' up there in the dark watchin' the sea. Ye get a grand view from my window. I like watchin' the lights on the big ships far out, wonderin' where they're bound. Sometimes I have a wile longin' on me to be on board one o' them an' get away to hell from all this. D'ye ever have that sort of wantin' on ye, Annie?'

She did not reply. He turned to look at her and sighed.

'Ah well, no use dreamin' about things that'll never be. 'Tis the oul' dog for the hard road an' the pup for the boreen. Here's where I am an' here's where I'll die, I've no doubt.'

He looked at her again.

'Can't seem to settle this weather.'

He stood on the doorstep, one arm around her shoulder and seemed to be listening though the night and the sea made no sound.

Then he said abruptly, ushering her into the kitchen, 'Come on away in. Sit there in my chair. It's the comfortablest. I'll stir the fire an' ye can make us a drop of hot punch. Nothin' like a drop of hot punch for the talkin' or the sleepin',' and he took a bottle of John Power from the cupboard and set it and the blue-ringed sugar bowl on the middle of the table.

'For Mary,' she said, propping the letter against his wife's silver-framed picture on the dresser, before throwing her coat on the sofa and filling a jug full of water from the white enamel bucket into the kettle and swinging it over the fire.

He stared at the envelope where it sat. Her back was to him when he lifted it and slid it into his pocket, eyes lingering on the framed face behind it.

'Aye nothin' like a drop o' hot punch of a winter's evenin' to settle a body. I even knew a fella who tried two o' them an' he's still alive,' he laughed, easing himself into the other armchair as the kettle began to whistle steam.

'Now, what have they been up to while I was away?'

Six

As the wind filled the jib of the little sloop, Brendon moved her over to the Rineen side, slipping down the long estuary and out into the Atlantic towards the dark mass of Horse Island, barely visible against a slightly less black horizon. Cloud obscured the stars and moon but the rain had ceased and with it the fog had thinned to a light mist. He cursed under his breath. Why couldn't it last till the job was done? For even so late in the year, the dawn would be upon him around half past six o'clock, some four hours away.

He had rounded the Black Rock off the tip of the island now and as he tried to penetrate the thick night for the bulky shape, a single momentary pinprick of light flashed away to his right for the merest second and he pulled the rudder hard to port, steering for its intermittent flicker. The mainsail filled and the *Northern Star* fairly danced over the modest waves, and in ten minutes, with a practised skill beyond his years, he was turning full into the breeze and gliding neatly alongside the grey hull and hooking onto the chains with scarcely a bump. Foreign-tongued whispers came from high over his head.

'Bold Fenian Men,' replied Brendon quietly and almost at once heard the boxes scraping against the steel of the freighter's side as the two coffin-sized crates were lowered on creaking davits. Carefully he guided them into his hold, almost filling it totally.

'Change in plans, my young friend, 'came an officer's voice from higher up, abaft on the bridge, spoken in strongly accented but perfectly understandable English. 'Rosscarbery Pier. The other is watched.'

Brendon stared up at the dark silhouette.

'But Skipper, my instructions are for Spanish Head,' he began but the answer came back quickly and with the authority of a ship's Master used to giving orders.

'Rosscarbery Pier! Good luck.'

'Same to you, Captain,' replied Brendon shrugging his shoulders in resignation. It was nothing to him. One place was as good as another so long as he was met, and the new rendezvous was closer. He could be back all the sooner. He slid the hatches back into place and tied down the canvas covers. Without another word, he unhooked and moved away along the hull and, running before the wind now, passed Tra Na Marbh, the Beach of the Dead, getting its name from where coffins were brought ashore for the priest's blessing when the island was inhabited by more than sheep. Then he stood well out across Union Hall Harbour, where, as the story was told, Nelson's body, embalmed in rum, first made landfall after Trafalgar in this very same month just a hundred and fifteen years before. He headed for Glandor Point, some four miles away. A few early or late fishermen's lighted windows in the small village and some deliberately illuminated cottages on the port beam kept him on course, though truth to tell he could have navigated that shore blindfolded.

He was too intent on his mission and its successful conclusion to look back, but even if he had it would have been impossible to make out the low silhouette of the rowing boat, two men on the oars, slipping away from behind the freighter's long, curved, steel hull before its engines began to rumble into life and it eased away South into the Atlantic and its Mediterranean destination.

'A good night's work I do be thinkin',' hissed one of the men as they were swallowed up in the darkness, heading in the opposite direction towards Toe Head and the small cave beneath the cliff, only accessed by water.

''Tis true for ye,' answered his companion. 'Now it's only us an' himself knows the pick-up spot an' only you an' me knows of the wee change in cargo.'

Brendon turned his craft well out to sea as was his wont, lest unfriendly, prying eyes of whatever hue were keeping watch. This doubled his journey but kept him away from hidden rocks till a couple of hours later the fog had given way totally to a thin autumn mist and a gibbous hunter's moon was casting a pale sheen into the comforting darkness. He could just make out the shape of the Church of Ireland Cathedral, halfway up the hill as he tacked in towards his destination. He unclicked the mainsail stays and gathered it onto the roof of the small wheelhouse. Keeping close in under the shadow of the low cliffs, he dropped the jib fifty yards out and coasted easily on the flowing tide to the small, stone famine pier which served the Rosscarbery fishermen, half a mile from the town.

Every nerve was as taut as his sails had been minutes before. He scanned the laneway down from the high road and the sandy shores of the narrow inlet leading right up under the village itself. There was nothing. No lights shone and no bird called. Only the gurgle of the sea along the dressed granite stones made any sound. It was just too quiet. Surely someone should have been there to meet him. It was far too risky to hang about there for long. Where the hell were they? He eased the boat along to the steps, grabbed the iron ring and passed his bow-line through, hastily knotting it in a highwayman's-hitch for easy escape. Still no sound caught his ears, straining and alert for the slightest click or studded boot on rock. Carefully he mounted the stair and stood erect on the little jetty, breathing heavily. There was a rustle from a bush behind him.

'Just don't move a single Irish muscle,' came a voice. 'Stand exactly as you are, rebel, if you want to draw another breath.'

Truth to tell, Brendon could not have moved even if he had dared. From over the weather-break-wall across the lane, half a dozen dark figures, rifle bolts clicking in unison, rose and stood silhouetted against the failing moon. The same Lieutenant walked forward, Smith and Wesson dangling loosely from its trigger guard.

'Dead to rights, Brendy, what? Cuffs, corporal! Johnston, Wright, just step down and let's see what pretty boy has brought us. Fish, Brendy?'

Brendon was gathering his wits once more. He knew he was lucky to be still alive for these ruffians didn't need much provocation to put a bullet in him and often had served others thus for far less than this. He glanced around for any avenue of escape before the handcuffs were snapped on his wrists. A dash for the end of the quay, a dive, and then what? He wouldn't get five yards without a dozen bullets ripping open his back and anyway, as he knew only too well, it was founded on a jumble of rocks stretching far into the water. Talk! Say something! Anything.

'That's right, Lieutenant,' he said. 'Fish. I go out to meet the French drifters and they're only too glad to sell me a few cram at dirt prices. Easier than tryin' to catch them meself.'

'Oh I see you are a little more respectful now, Brendy,' smiled the officer. 'It's not "bunch of thugs" this time, eh? Still, it's a goodly yarn. I love Irish yarns. Fish, eh?'

He laughed, poking the lad in the stomach with the revolver.

'Hurry up lads,' he called down. 'I want to take a look at these lovely herrings. Maybe I'll have a few for my breakfast, what?'

Brendon could hear the hatches being dragged back and the boxes raised and dumped on the small afterdeck.

'Use your bayonet there, Johnston. Get that lid off. I'm dying to have a fish for my breakfast,' and he laughed again.

In his shackles, Brendon closed his eyes and prayed to the Holy Virgin that they might bring him to Dublin Castle at least. There he might have some chance of a trial, but oh how often had he heard of 'Shot while trying to escape', and the Tans were the lads to do it. With regular army or the Royal Irish Constabulary, he might have had a chance of simple arrest but not this bunch of uniformed criminals.

'Fish, Lieutenant, 'called up Johnston. 'Full of fuckeen fish!'

'Fish, my arse,' snapped the officer. 'That's only on top. Stick the bayonets in, man. Hurry.'

The boy could smell the sweet odour of herring rising up and closed his eyes in another prayer to the Beloved Mother of Jesus. A mistake! A mistake! Yes the sailors had given him the wrong cases. Oh dear God, could it be that!

'No sir,' called Wright. 'Fish all the way through and this one is the fuckeen same. Just fuckeen fish!'

'Search the rest of the boat,' roared the Lieutenant and Brendon could see in the gathering light his white teeth grinding in frustrated anger. 'Take it apart. They're here somewhere. You two get down there and help. The Irish whelp has them fucking somewhere. Just find the fucking rifles. I don't give a continental damn if you wreck it!' And they almost did just that.

An hour later, the handcuffs were unlocked none too gently.

'I know there's something going on here, fancy boy,' said the Lieutenant, 'and by the Sweet Jesus, I'll get to the bottom of it yet.'

He shoved the barrel of his .45 hard under the lad's chin, adding quietly, 'And I warn you, don't come out with any of your smart remarks for I'm just in the right mood to wipe any grinning from that pretty face of yours.'

He turned away, holstering his revolver and buttoning down the safety strap.

'Some of you fill a couple of those buckets with fish. We might as well come away with something.'

For some moments, as Johnston and his mate lifted bailers from the ruined floor and filled them with silver fish, the Lieutenant stared at the scene, deep in thought, then, without looking back, started up the lane muttering more to himself than his company, 'Even the fucking leaders of the rabble don't know what they're at. So much for their fucking Intelligence!'

For a very long time after the roar of their Crossley had left the main road, Brendon sat on the bollard, his whole body trembling and his mind in a whirl. What the bloody hell was going on?

At last he roused himself and went down into the chaos of his beloved *Northern Star*. They had done a thorough job but at least they hadn't smashed the hull. Lockers, thwarts and the two small bunks had been torn out, the cabin floor lay in a pile of loose planks and the wheelhouse was a shambles.

It was full dawn with a beautiful golden sun coming up over the distant Galley Head below Clonakilty before he eased her out on the jib and limped back to Castletownshend. He tied up and trudged slowly up the steep hill, past

Heggerty's Bar and the sleeping house. Slipping quietly in the unlocked door of the cottage, he heard the gentle snoring from his aunt's room as he dropped his clothes to the floor and crawled exhausted into his bed.

Seven

It seemed he had only been asleep for minutes when his door was rapped and, putting her head round it, his aunt said, 'You did come back then. I thought I heard you come in. Come on. Breakfast's ready. Are you going to lie there all day? Lobsters can get back outo' pots when the sun's on them, ye know. They'll not wait around just for you.'

It was minutes before the previous night's adventure flashed back to him in all its detail and as he splashed cold water on his face in the big ceramic bowl on the washstand before dressing, he marvelled at his escape and pondered the source of his cargo. If the sailors hadn't made a genuine mistake, just what the hell was going on? He entered the kitchen and sat down at the table before one of his aunt's delicious fries.

She sat opposite him with a cup of tea warming her hands, eyes never leaving his face, while he eagerly attacked the sausage, eggs and bacon, reaching for a slice of fried bread from the plate in front of him.

'Well?' she asked when her curiosity could be contained no longer.

He looked up innocently.

'Well what, Aunty?' he said wide-eyed and she swiped him across the side of his head with the drying cloth beside her.

'What happened, you spalpeen?' she said, smiling across at him, the sun from the window shining her hair into a golden halo, and not for the first time he thought she was a right pretty woman, just like her sister, his mother, had been.

'You, Brendon, are the agravatinest nephew I ever had. Tell me what happened last night and why are ye back?'

'I, dear Aunty, am the only aggravatin' nephew you have, in case you hadn't noticed,' he answered, laughing, and then went on to tell her about the close call he had had.

'God, Aunt Annie, I was never as glad to smell a herring in my life. Some mistake on the freighter, I suppose, God bless their wee brown Arab hides.'

For a long time she sat, sipping her tea and pondering his tale.

'Aye,' she said at last. 'That must have been what happened, but let that be the last. You can't be so lucky all the time. That's twice. See there isn't a third, Brendon. Your Fairy Godmother might not be around the next time. My nerves can't stick it an' ye never know when young Lieutenant Brown might be replaced for someone not so principled.'

He glanced up at her, spluttering through a mouthful of bacon.

'Principled?' he queried. 'Principled? By the Holy Mother, Aunty, 'tis not a word you'd use if you faced the bugger like I did last night with his revolver stuck under your chin. He was just itchin' to show me how good he was with that forty-five of his. Principled?'

His aunt said nothing, staring down into her tea. He drained his mug and wiped his mouth with the back of his hand and, picking up his tool-kit, left her sitting there, deep in thought.

'See you!' he called as he closed the front door behind him and made his way down to the harbour.

It was well into the afternoon before he had checked and re-baited his pots with stinking rotten fish by borrowing Mr Heggerty's small rowing boat and had made a goodly start on his repairs, which weren't as bad as he had first thought. Although they had ripped out the timber, they had actually broken very little and much of it was easily nailed or screwed back into position. Suddenly he straightened from his task.

'Good God!' he exclaimed, startling several seagulls which rose screeching out over the West Quay. 'My note! Mary!'

He dropped the hammer and, grabbing his windbreaker started up the hill.

Mary, green eyes smiling under her thick dark curls, greeted him on the doorstep.

'You're early, sweetheart. We have hours yet. The Cork train doesn't leave till eight. I'm all packed and ready. Will your uncle in Macroom meet us in Bandon? I'm so excited to be going at last.'

'My note!' exclaimed Brendon, quite out of breath. 'I thought you'd have been away. My note!'

'Note? What note? I got no note.'

'Well thank God for that anyway,' he answered. 'I thought you'd have been gone. I said in the note!'

'What note, Brendon?' she asked again getting slightly irritated. 'There was no note.'

'Is your father at home?' Brendon asked suddenly cutting her short, some sort of light starting to penetrate his thoughts for he was sure his aunt would have delivered it. 'Was he at the fishin' last night?'

'No to both questions,' she said. 'He's not in and he was not fishin' last night. When he got back from Cork, he sat in that chair like a zombie all evenin' and wouldn't speak, just suckin' that stinkin' pipe. Then he would walk outside and stand, staring out to sea. He seemed to be sort of listenin' for somethin'.

'Och I dunno. I was glad when it was my bedtime. For the first night in weeks, I was asleep as soon as my head hit the pillow. I dunno what time he went up. Then this mornin' after he had his breakfast, he said he had to finish yesterday's business in Cork City and would be away overnight. That's all I was told. Even Michaeleen was lookin' for him but had to go out alone. Brendon, what is this all about?'

For a long time the lad looked into those clear, emerald, trusting eyes. He took her hand and led her inside to the sofa and they sat down.

'Brendon! What is it, Brendon? What's the matter?'

'We can't go today, my love,' he said softly. She began to protest but he covered her lips with his before repeating almost in a whisper, 'We can't go just yet, Mary, for there are things to be done. Don't ask me, Mary. There are things to be done: loose ends need tyin' up. I'm not havin' them houndin' me down for the rest of my life as an informer and me innocent but I promise on my mother's grave that as soon as it's settled, we'll be off. A few days. A week at most. The packet doesn't leave Cork till the end of the month. Trust me, sweetheart. It has to be.

'I can't leave just yet, not till I get a few things cleared up around here. If I don't get it settled, we could be runnin' for the rest of our lives. They have mighty long memories and as surely, longer arms. Even after years they never give up an' I'm not bringin' that on ye, Mary.' He held her tightly but the eyes staring over her shoulder were deep in morbid thought.

'But Brendon,' she began, tears welling in those eyes but he kissed her again.

'You know I cannot be tellin' you,' he said. 'It's better you know nothin'. I think you understand that. I'll be back this evenin'. He'll be out?'

'He's always out,' she sniffed. 'Last night was a wonder itself.'

Later that same afternoon, as he nailed, mended and replaced planks down at the pier, Brendon's mind was in a whirl. From time to time tourists would stand and watch or even ask what happened but they were few and far between in those troubled days so mostly he was left to his own devices and distinctly uncomfortable conclusions.

'How's it comin', Brendon?'

He looked up into the grim face of Michaeleen.

For more than a minute they stared into each others eyes, then the older man, taking the pipe from his mouth and glancing around at the few stragglers far away enough not to hear said, 'So ye ran into trouble, last night! There's debriefin' to be done. Heggerty's around nine. Up the Castle wood and in the back. Be sure nobody sees ye for there's them in this village that's fierce good at puttin' two an' two together – aye an' at least one in particular. Not a word to anyone, 'specially to Mary. Lives depend on it, lad.'

He struck a light to his pipe, flicked the match into the water, blew a cloud of white smoke into the fading afternoon and strolled over to the edge of the quay to watch with a fisherman's eye the cat's-paw of a rising mackerel shoal towards the Eastern shore.

They were in the gloom of the back kitchen behind the bar, three pints sitting in front of them. Brendon had made his report in every detail. Neither man interrupted him but from time to time during the tale, they glanced at each other, nodding significantly. Then Michaeleen spoke.

'Ye see, Brendon, the informer couldn't have been you for—', and here he gave a little apologetic clearing of the throat, 'ye were close watched from when ye left here that night and of course, as ye know, a double check was the changing of the rendezvous out at sea and only the Army Council knew that. We had a Volunteer lyin' hid above the inlet at Spanish Head in case it was you an' somehow you had slipped our man, passed on your destination an' the soldiers were waitin' there. There was nobody below Clon so the conclusion is obvious.'

'So ye see we knew it wasn't you,' went on Heggerty. 'Oh because of my feelin's for your aunt, I always leaned to that fact but it had to be proved beyond doubt and in quick time too; nor could we afford to lose the consignment. The reasons don't matter to you but we had to know before the end of the month.'

Michaeleen raised a hand as Brendon would have spoken, anger rising in him as he realised the full meaning of what he was hearing. They had actually thought he was a traitor and had laid a trap for him! He rose, his face flaming.

'You actually thought it was me?' he shouted, forgetting the customers the other side of the wall. 'You thought—'

'Come on, lad,' said Michaeleen. 'Sit down and keep yer voice down as well. You know these things have to be done in a war situation. We had to know. Surely ye can see that.'

'But me!' cried Brendon in a more moderate voice. 'Me that takes all the risks! Me that—'

'Easy, lad,' interrupted Heggerty. 'That'll do. Neither Michaeleen nor I had any doubts about you but there's more to this than you know. Just leave it. You're innocent and there's an end of it.'

The boy would have said more but Michaeleen raised his hand again.

'No, Brendon,' he said. 'No questions. Just know that we fixed the Skipper to give you the new destination, the one only the Council knew, an' the boxes we brought out. We were on the opposite side of the freighter as ye loaded the fish. Aye an' as sure as wee apples we wouldn't be talkin' to you tonight if we hadn't. Ye'd have been so much dead meat on Rosscarbery Pier, else. Those bastards take no prisoners, Brendon, you know that an' what's more, the consignment would have been lost as well as you.'

'Aye but how did they know I'd be there?' asked the boy. 'Who would have—'

His voice trailed away as his afternoon conversation with Mary and his deepening doubts rushed back and he stared, wide-eyed at them.

'Yes,' said Michaeleen watching his face in the flickering firelight. 'Yes, an' Mary tells me he's away to Cork for a few days. Aye an' never a word to me, his partner. Convenient?'

'Oh my God,' breathed Brendon, holding his head in his hands. 'It can't be. God, no. It just can't. It'll kill Mary. Surely there's some other explanation?'

The faces of the two men across the table were grim and silent. The boy stared from one to the other searching for some glimmer of a change of mind but there was none.

'Can't be any doubt, not after last night,' said Heggerty. 'I can think of only one other remote possibility but that's between Michaeleen an' me an' we'll thrash it out in our own time.'

Michaeleen leaned back in his chair, rubbing a hand over his eyes.

'We first suspected it months ago. You know he fancies your aunt of course? Well for that reason he tried to frame Heggerty here but failed there too.'

'Frame you, Mr Heggerty?' asked Brendon without understanding.

'Oh before your time lad,' said the publican. 'Back just after the '16 Easter Risin'. Och I had a few old single-shot rifles with ammunition an a half dozen Mills bombs in the shed out back but thanks to your aunt, I got rid of them just in time. I dunno how she knew but the very next day the Auxies took this place apart. You know they're nearly as bad when they find nothin' as when they do. Ye can still see the cracks in the panellin' inside in the bar. I thought they might burn the place down round my ears for badness but the Sergeant stopped them. Not a bad man, the Sergeant. He's a Cork man o' course. Born an' raised in Ballydehobb direction I believe. Anyway that's the story an' I have yer Aunt Annie to thank for the warnin' an' I have me own notion where she wheedled it from but I never asked her.'

Brendon sat in stunned silence and lifted his glass. It was barely believable. He could make a fair guess himself for he knew Mary's father had a notion of the fair lady too and was brave and fond of a sup.

'*In vino veritas*,' he smiled but the two faces remained blank for their Latin was limited to a few phrases from the Sunday Mass.

'Well you and your association with his Mary were next,' went on Michaeleen, taking up the tale without comment. 'A handy way of getting someone else to do the dirty on you and so keep his daughter no better than a servant girl. You should have been shot that last time but you were too quick for them. We four were the only ones to know that destination an' of course you were the obvious informer because you got away. He had two chances, ye see. Either the Tans got ye or a court martial an' summary execution. The result would have been the same, don't you see.'

'Aye an' if we hadn't changed the boxes, he'd have had his way this time at Rosscarbery Pier,' commented Heggerty. 'Now we're almost a hundred percent sure but just in case can you remember anything to make it a hundred and one? For we daren't be makin' mistakes, not with a life at stake. Did the Lieutenant say anything, anything at all that might . . .'

Brendon looked to the low ceiling, casting his mind back to those terrifying minutes on the small quay, only eighteen hours previously. There was something, something somewhere at the back of his mind. He had noticed it at the time but—

'Yes! Yes! That's it. Yeah! There was one remark,' he began. 'When they found nothing but fish and nothin' in the boat, he said to the corporal something like, ah what was it exactly, ah, "So much for the fucking brains of the rabble. Even the fucking leaders don't know what's going on." Yeah! It was that or somethin' like it. He definitely mentioned leaders and the Intelligence of the rabble. Yes, that was it. I wondered about that. That's what it was. I noted it at the time but I had more to think about than that. Remember I was still in danger of bein' shot just out of crookedness.'

'I know, I know,' said Michaeleen. 'The Intelligence; the leaders! Hmm. That'll do. That'll do just fine. Now you gather up your things and your Mary and get to hell away from this village. Leave the rest to us. It'll be better if yis are both far away in the next few days. Go now, Brendon. Leave the rest to us. We'll see the word on you gets to the right ears. No suspicion will hang on you and at least you can console yourself that I'm sure of one thing. He didn't do it for money an' I'd swear once the pair of you have gone out of reach, it mayn't happen again.'

'Aye Michaeleen,' said Heggerty, nodding thoughtfully, 'that may or may not be so, but this has to be dealt with an' soon at that. We can't take any risks or the whole unit could find themselves in Kilmainam, aye an' they would be the lucky ones!'

'But but I just can't believe it of him,' said Brendon. 'He wouldn't jeopardise a mission just to get me out of the way. I can't believe he hates me that much. There must be some other explanation. It has to be someone else.'

'Go now, Brendon,' said the publican. 'Go on, lad. We'll do what has to be done, but keep a very tight mouth on ye. Like an oyster, lad, and I know I needn't tell ye Mary must never know.'

Without another word, the youth departed with a heavy heart and his worst fears confirmed while the publican looked steadily at Michaeleen and tapped the panel in the wall.

Eight

It was a few days later. Heggerty and Michaeleen were early for the meeting when Mick came in.

'Sorry I'm late,' he said. 'Just back from Cork. A bit o' a problem over the deeds to the old house. Couldn't even sell an' oul' rickle o' stones wi'out forty forms to be signed an' stamped. O' course if it had bin an Englishman wanted it – a different story there I'll bet.'

He looked from one to the other.

'O'Boyle an' the Master?' he inquired.

'Baldy's supposed to be on watch at the head of the village an' the Master's at a school meetin'. Sent his apologies!'

'Well,' he asked, pulling up a chair. 'Report! What happened? Come on! What happened wi' the last run? Report!'

Michaeleen had just opened his mouth to reply when the outside kitchen door swung wide.

'Monaghan!' exclaimed the publican, springing to his feet. 'What the hell? Where the hell do you think you're goin'? The damned cheek!'

'That's enough,' snapped a voice behind the older man. 'He's only showin' me the way down the back. You know I can't be seen here. I got a lift to the Creamery an' expected one o' you to be there to meet me. Fortunately this gentleman was on his way here. Didn't ye get word I was comin'?'

He turned and thanked the small man with a cock-pheasant's feather in his grimy hat and shut the door after him.

'Is he all right?' the visitor asked, nodding at the door.

'Oh Monaghan's harmless,' replied Heggerty. 'He knows better than to talk anyway. Only interested in sheep an' stout.'

'Were ye not contacted?' asked the visitor.

'So much for O'Boyle,' said Mick, rising and offering his chair. 'We did have a man but he's over-fond of the crather. Lyin' asleep in the ditch somewhere. I'll need to have a word with that gent.'

'Never mind that now,' said the man, throwing off his heavy coat and sitting down. 'I'm here now an' I'm on a very tight schedule. I've no time to waste on your domestic problems.'

'This is Tom Barry, our Sub-District Commandant an' Intelligence Officer in the county,' introduced Mick. 'My two Lieutenants, Michaeleen and Seamus. Two good men.'

'I need six from here,' said Barry without acknowledging the greeting or preamble. 'Can you muster that? I've a bit more reconnoitring to do but it'll be the end of November. I have a man planted, never mind where for the present. He'll give me the exact date and time an' I'll get word to you. And in view of the report on things down here, it'll only be at the very last minute. There can be no slip-ups this time like that bloody fiasco last month in Kerry. Three good men dead because of a drunken whore with a mouth as big as her cunt an' an asshole who couldn't keep it in his breeches till he got home.'

His audience sat in silence for they too knew all about that fiasco outside Dingle.

He turned to Mick and continued in the tone of authority he had been using since entering the kitchen.

'You bring your catch to the Bandon Market every Thursday?'

Mick nodded.

'On Thursday the eighteenth you'll be met an' given the date. Did you succeed in getting the arms or was that another balls-up I'll have to sort out?'

'No balls-up,' replied Michaeleen indignantly. 'We got the whid of treachery an' we changed the venue. Complete success. Enough rifles an' to spare, safely stowed.'

He looked at Mick.

'You were away, Mick. Couldn't contact you in time. Took it upon ourselves to switch young Brendon's boxes for fish. We did the run ourselves.'

'Aye,' said Heggerty, carefully avoiding the variation in the original plan, 'an it was a damn good job we did. They were waitin' for him. If we hadn't, we'd have lost a good lad as well as the rifles.'

His tone was defiant, even in the face of this superior.

'We're already aware of that situation and the County Commandant says you're to deal with it yourselves,' Barry snapped irritably as if it were an irrelevance.

Heggerty looked up sharply. He wasn't going to be intimidated in his own pub.

'An' how did you know that?' he asked, for the situation was only some days old and there were no telephones in Castletownshend and only two in Skibbereen.

The blue-grey eyes bored into the publican's for long moments above a grim tight mouth.

'You can sort that out in your own time. I'll have nothin' disruptin' this operation! It's far too important. Clean up your own shit but see that you don't jeopardise this action or heads will roll an' it won't end at your informer,' he said, ignoring the question.

Michaeleen suddenly pictured the thin sharp-nosed face under the shining bald pate and thought maybe it was as well Mr Barry had missed O'Boyle. But his friend, Seamus, however couldn't get the lean, grey-stubbled chin beneath the cock-feathered hat out of his mind. Possibilities! Both men began to be busy with their private thoughts but Barry brought them back to the present.

'Have ye enough arms for yourselves and another half dozen? Rifles, mind!'

'We have. We have now. Safe an' sound, oiled and ready,' was the reply.

Mick was silent as he glanced at each in turn. Then he said, 'Well done, lads. Who gave ye the word?'

'I told ye that's your problem,' snapped Barry, cutting him short. 'You will have ways of dealin' with informers. I'm fryin' bigger fish altogether. You be sure you're there at the November Market.'

'Ammunition?' inquired Mick, turning his attention from his Lieutenants.

'You'll get it on route. Donovan's Hotel in Clonakilty sell fine breakfasts,' replied Barry shortly.

'How will I know the contact?' asked Mick.

'He'll know you,' was the curt reply. 'Now I have to get back into Skibbereen. I have a meetin' there before I catch the train to Cork. I have a man to meet on the way too. I'll need transport. Can ye manage that?'

'No problem,' said Mick rising and, with Barry nodding briefly to Michaeleen and Heggerty, they left the room.

The two sat staring at each other till they heard the old lorry starting and, with its ancient gears grinding, wheezing up the steep street. Then Michaeleen spoke, almost breathlessly. 'Jeesus!'

They sat down and the publican said quietly, 'Be jassus there's a cold shark if iver I saw one. Did ye see the eyes on him? I wouldn't want to be on the wrong side of that boy.'

'Aye,' replied Michaeleen, 'but more to the point, did our bold Commandant suspect that we know what we think we know? Did he swallow our story?'

'What the hell else could he do without exposin' himself? Of course he did.'

Heggerty rapped on the panel and, accompanied by a swelling of conversation and pipe smoke from the bar beyond, two more pints were pushed through the opening by young Kelly the part-time help and the panel slid back into place.

Michaeleen lifted his and drank it halfway down.

'Aye,' he said softly, 'but the whole bloody business is now left to us. He made that quite clear an' mind, this is a very small village that knows every move of each other. Hmm, Seamus. We're the ones dropped in the shit now, as himself put it an' we're the ones who have to live here, not Mr Bloody Barry.'

They drank in silence, both knowing what had to be done but neither having any stomach for the deed. Then Heggerty said, considering each word: 'Listen, Michaeleen, is there any way we could get a message directly to the County Commandant. As you said, this is far too small a village. We need an outsider. Barry seems to know *but I'd rather go right to the top.*'

His companion studied his tankard.

'Hmm. Leave it with me, Seamus. Leave it with me. I'll think o' somethin'.'

Nine

Mick dropped his passenger and rattled away across the Market yard and out onto Townshend Street, while Barry strolled casually along between darkened shop windows and was soon pushing aside a beaded curtain covering the back room door at his second rendezvous.

Half an hour later, just as nonchalantly he returned along the deserted pavement and turned down the hill to the Skibbereen Station. Inside, he stamped his feet on the small platform, whistling as he waited for the train from Baltimore with his hands deep in heavy black coat, for the November night was turning chill and foggy. His tune, 'The Bold Fenian Men', drifted down the empty station to the old man who hummed in unison in his small ticket office.

He was quite contented with his evening's work. O'Brien had been as good as his word and had gathered half a dozen men into the back of the small pub in North Street. They still needed the rifles from Castletownshend but Mick had assured him they were in hand and would be delivered well in time. The men themselves had been alert and keen. They were anxious to know the nature and location but Barry had said in that flat humourless tone of his, 'All in good time men. You'll be told all in good time. There seems to be a rat at the malt somewhere in this district so the less you know, the better. Suffice to say, the operation is goin' ahead. Don't worry. You'll be contacted after the Bandon Market.'

Two RIC men strolled at their regulation two and a half miles per hour along the footpath and turned in at the station door, more in search of a bit of shelter from the cold wind than in any pursuit of duty. Their large silver helmet badges glistened in the massive, circular, brass oil lamp hanging from the girdered vault of the roof. They stopped in front of him.

'I don't know you,' said the one with the heavy moustache. 'Name?'

'Barry. Thomas Barry.'

'You're not from around here.' It was a statement, not a question, for the Police knew everyone in those days.

'Where are ye from, Thomas?' asked the other.

'Cork City,' he replied.

'A bit off yer pad?' inquired the Constable. 'What brings ye away down to these parts?'

'Down makin' a lobster deal with Mick McCarthy an' payin' a few bills. Ye have to keep payin' the piper or ye'll get no tune, ye know Sergeant.'

'Hmm,' said moustache. 'I'm partial to a bit of lobster meself. Hmm.'

Barry had a strange feeling this was not going to be the end of the conversation but just as the sweat began to break at the back of his neck, a mournful 'toot toot toot' echoed along the Mardyke steep walls and with a rattle and scream of brakes the Baltimore to Cork train, with its small engine and three carriages, belched into the station. Reverentially he touched the rim of his bowler hat, stepped smartly round the Law and dropped into the empty third class compartment and slammed the heavy door gratefully behind him.

Hurrying from his ticket office, the old man, well aware of the developing situation on his platform, hastily gave a shrill blast on his whistle, green flag waving furiously at the driver watching from his cab, and immediately, with a hiss of steam and a skidding of wheels, it rumbled hollowly across the small wooden bridge over the Ilen River, leaving the two Policemen staring after its red tail-light, disappearing into the November fog.

As he trundled along the coast, with glimpses of the white wave crests away on his right when the mist billowed and lifted now and then, his mind planned and re-planned his moves so that the sudden braking as they ran into Clonakilty took him by surprise. The carriage door opened and a large heavily coated man climbed in and with a sigh, lowered himself onto the cushion opposite.

'How did it go, Jim? Any trouble?'

James O'Sullivan shook his head.

'Sweet as a nut, Tom,' he answered. 'Sweet as a nut. Seven ready an' willin'.'

'Grand! Grand!' answered Barry. 'Townshend think they have an informer but the rifles and men are ready. I told them to sort out their own problems. We daren't let anything get in the way of this operation. I can't be sure how long my man can remain in Macroom Castle without bein' discovered. He tells me he thinks he's bein' watched.'

He paused, staring out of the window he'd wiped condensation from, then continued. 'This'll strike a blow for Ireland that will be talked about in a hundred years, Jim. A hundred years!'

They sat, each engrossed in his own thoughts though no doubt on the same subject, its risks, its chances of success and, not least, the aftermath. If they were successful, they were both aware that the Authorities would wreak a terrible vengeance and if they were not, how many of them would be going home. Some nineteen miles and thirty minutes later, the little train wheezed into Bandon. Barry let down the window on its leather strap and filled the space, deterring other passengers from entering, but he needn't have bothered. The one traveller came forward, was admitted and the window raised.

'Well, Deasy?' was the curt welcome and it was obvious that there was no love lost.

'All fixed up,' came the equally short reply as the new man nodded to O'Sullivan.

'All right, Jim?'

'Doin' the best, Pat. Bad oul' night.'

'I suppose they have no arms?' cut in Barry.

'A couple of revolvers and an old muzzle-loader,' replied Deasy.

'The Townshend men assure me that they have enough for everybody,' said Barry. 'They'll be got to you after the eighteenth. It'll be up to you to get them distributed and see you don't make a havers of it like the last time.'

The man opened his mouth to protest but Barry silenced him with a steady glare, then turned to the other man.

'Same for you, Jim. I'll want it all done by the twentieth. It has to be done by that date at the latest an' yer platoons billeted within walkin' distance from Gleann Chapel.'

O'Sullivan would have asked a question but Barry raised a hand.

'That's all at the moment, Jim. I still have a bit of reconnoitring to do before I pick the most suitable spot but that's where I want you all by the twentieth or even a day before if you can manage it. Get that word to your local Commandants but no more. Just that.'

Again they lapsed into silence as they trundled through the mist-damped dark towards Cork City and their separate ways and occupations.

Ten

It was cold, drizzly and boot-black at six in the morning when the old Ford lorry left the quay in Castletownshend and panted up the steep hill past the four trees. Michaeleen and Mick didn't talk much on the journey, turning right above the chapel to cut out Skibbereen and pass through Leap, Rosscarbery, and into Clonakilty. A grey dawn paled the sky ahead as they entered the little town and squeezed the rattling vehicle down the narrow entry into the yard at the back of Donavan's Hotel.

'A pint an' a pie?' asked Michaeleen. 'That'll put us in Bandon about half eight.'

The back door opened into a low-ceilinged bar with tables and snugs along one wall. Many of these were occupied already, even at this hour, with others on their way to the Market or indeed some just getting a little liquid fortification before opening their several premises for business. The two pint-sippers in the corner, though, for all their plain clothes, stuck out like sore thumbs as a pair of detectives on a listening brief. They gave their order to the bleary-eyed son of the house leaning on the counter. He called it through a hatch behind him and while they waited for the food, took their drinks to a booth that was unoccupied. They sat back, filling pipes and surveying their companions. In a few minutes, a tall young redhead drained his glass and, in making for the door, stopped by their table.

'Top o' the mornin', gents,' he said without in any way trying to lower his voice. 'Call in at the shop on the way. I have that bridle mended, good as new. All right?'

'Right ye be,' answered Mick, without a moment's hesitation. 'Pick it up in twenty minutes or so.'

The hot pork pies arrived accompanied by yesterday's potatoes, crisply fried in bacon fat, and it was only when they had gratefully finished them off, paid the bill and then stopped outside the saddlers for a couple of minutes while Redhead threw an old sack into the back among the boxes of fish and they were leaving the town that Michaeleen asked, 'Who was that?'

'No idea,' returned Mick from the driver's seat. 'Not an idea in the wide world. Doesn't even work for Lawson, the saddler, but I'll wager our load is completed now.'

They were only three or four miles beyond the town when suddenly Mick's whistle stopped in mid-note.

'Jeesus,' he exclaimed through clenched teeth as the red light made a circle in the dark some twenty yards ahead and then waved from side to side.

'Easy, Mick,' said Michaeleen softly, putting a hand on his arm as his partner double declutched and, with the aid of his grinding gears, brought the old lorry shuddering to a halt, only feet from the Black and Tan patrol.

The Sergeant strolled forward, a man either side of him with rifle at the high port, while three others lowered their weapons and lounged against their armoured car, drawn across the road, a few yards ahead. Mick wound down his window.

'Name?' was the curt command.

'McCarthy,' answered Mick. 'Mick McCarthy from Castletownshend.'

'You?' and the light shone full on Michaeleen.

'Michaeleen Carey, also from Castletownshend.'

'Where are ye for, Michaeleen and Mick,' asked the soldier. 'A bit early for a mornin' jaunt? What's in the back?'

'Fish for the Market in Bandon,' answered Mick, sweat beginning to break around his collar as he remembered the sack, casually slung on by the saddler but in the same moment Michaeleen had his door thrown open and was stepping into the road.

'Take a look, Sergeant,' he invited coolly. 'Some of the finest mackerel and cod ye'll taste this side of Dublin.'

As he spoke, he put a foot on the back wheel and sprang into the rear. In a minute, he had opened the hasp on a couple of boxes and was lifting out some of his catch, while his foot was shoving the Hessian sack of ammunition back into a corner behind one of them.

'Take a look, McClean,' ordered the Sergeant and one of the patrol vaulted lightly over the tailboard. With his bayonet, he speared the open boxes and turned to a third.

'Ah laubsthers, Sarge,' he exclaimed in broad Glaswegian. 'Gran' big laubsters aye an' them stull scrawin' aboot, ye ken.'

'I would rather you took some cod instead,' said Michaeleen, standing where he was against the back of the cab. 'We've cod to spare but the lobsters is a special order. Here, why not some o' these fresh prawns?' and he helpfully dragged a box over the bag of bullets and threw up the lid. 'They're gran' big juicy fellas.'

'Roighto, McClean,' laughed the Sergeant, ignoring Michaeleen. 'A special order for a special patrol, eh? Take three and a couple of big cod. Oi just loves a nice piece o' cod wi' me chips. Should maike us right poplar in the mess. Anythin' else there?'

'Naw, Sarge,' replied the soldier, more interested in wrapping up his purloin in one of the old newspapers they always brought for that very purpose. 'Jist yer wee fishes. No as guid as Arbroth Smokies but they'll do jist fine, ye ken. Mick a nice change fray bully fuckin' beef!'

He climbed down and Michaeleen re-fastened his boxes with deliberate unhurried care letting them get well clear before following and heaving himself back into the cab as the patrol stood aside and waved them onto the grass verge, around the car partially blocking the narrow road.

'God, you're a cool one,' said Mick admiringly, taking care not to drive too fast away from them. 'I watched it in the mirror. Well done.'

'Cheap at the price,' replied his companion settling himself comfortably down in his seat and reaching into his pocket for his pipe and pouch. 'Sorry about the lobsters, though; the black enamel feckers,' and they drove on in contemplative silence.

The sun was well up and the day promised fine as the old lorry growled past the pound field, well occupied with draught horses, ponies and donkeys contentedly grazing after their early morning journeys, and nosed its way into Bandon Market yard.

Fruit and vegetables of every kind and hue were spilling from carts, shafts reaching skyward: pigs squealed and chickens squawked on every hand and women called their knit-wares, jams and breads from flat barrows with raucous ribaldry to each other and customer alike. Michaeleen and Mick waved to friends and acquaintances here and there as they slowly made their way to the Fish Corner.

They parked against a granite wall, threw down the side of the lorry and opened their catch, Mick taking care to shove the sack under the driver's seat first. Around them, transports of all shapes and sizes, from cut-down Model T's to panniered bicycles and hand-barrows were lined up with herrings, mackerel, whiting and cod glistening from half-opened boxes, waiting for the merchants from Cork City and beyond as far as Fermoy and Mitchellstown, Dunmanway and Macroom.

It was noon with most of their catch sold – fish being cheap and wholesome, more or less selling themselves – when the shortish broad, bowler-hatted dealer approached, slapping his riding crop against brown leather boots.

'An' a fine day to the pair of you, gentlemen,' he greeted. 'How many lobsters have ye there?'

Michaeleen looked up into the cold, steel-blue eyes that had so held him in Heggerty's kitchen, staring straight into his.

'All done, sir, today, but how many would ye be wantin'?' asked Mick without hesitation. 'We can easily get them for ye.'

The man tipped his hat to the back of his head, thinking as he studied the patches of blue sky between the scudding cotton-wool clouds.

'I'd need half a dozen. I supply all over an' there's a big weddin' comin' off near Clogher before the end of the month. Clogher! Och ye know it. Not far from Macroom. Oh nothin' but lobster'll do for the starter. Any chance ye could have them before this day week? I'd need them a few days before that.'

'I think I can manage that,' replied Mick, 'though ye don't give a body much time.'

'Round the twenty-first then,' said the man turning away. 'I'll be here. Oh if ye happen to be takin' a bite before ye go back, I can recommend the

Munster Arms. Grand Irish stew, thruppence a bowl an' a big yard for parkin' behind. Even a hayshed against any bad weather!'

'See ye, then,' said Mick easily, turning away to sling empty boxes onto the lorry a few yards behind.

'There's a price list anyway,' said Michaeleen softly, shoving a crumpled piece of paper into the immaculate, crimson riding-jacket pocket.

'Good luck to ye,' said their dealer without batting an eye and strolled away across the Market, towards a big chestnut mare, patiently cropping the grass by the gate, where a Policeman stood chatting with a Tan patrol.

Mick looked over at his companion.

'I could just massacre a bowl of that stew, Michaeleen. You?'

A quarter of an hour later the lorry was parked under cover in the yard of the Munster Arms and the two men were dipping thickly buttered chunks of fresh bread into their bowls and savouring the thick neck-of-mutton stew.

'The old Ford'll be a bit lighter on the way home,' remarked Michaeleen as he glanced out the window at the two jaunting cars clopping into the yard and making for the shed.

'True for ye an' damn the Tan we'll see ye may be sure,' answered Mick. 'Another bowl? We've plenty o' time.'

The lorry, relieved of its fish and cargo from the extended spare-wheel compartment under the body, fairly bounced its way home, with Mick driving the whole way this time in high good humour, whistling a tuneless 'Banks of My Own Lovely Lee' while Michaeleen swayed beside him, deep in thought and in spite of the rough mostly unmetalled roads they reached Castletownshend just as the light was fading.

'A pint, Mick?' asked Michaeleen, but his companion declined.

'I'll get home,' he said. 'I've things to see te an' Mary'll have the tea ready.'

Michaeleen climbed down and watched as his partner eased the old lorry down the steep hill, rounded the trees and tooted as he passed back up home.

He turned and pushed open the half door of Heggerty's pub.

'All sold?' asked the publican looking up from his glass-polishing.

'Done and dusted,' replied Michaeleen as the brimming pint slid along the bar to the end where he stood.

'It's time ye were away home, Monaghan,' said Heggerty to the only other occupant. 'Maggie'll have the spuds ready. Off wi' ye now. See ye later on.'

The man's mouth tightened and his eyes narrowed but he dutifully drained his glass, pulled down his red cock-feathered hat and, with a nod to Michaeleen, left the bar without a word.

'It was himself,' said the latter. 'Bold as brass in full ridin' gear with a big hunter tied at the gate. He asked for lobsters! The twenty-first. Three days. He wants six. Assembly point: Clogher.'

'The rifles?' asked Heggerty.

'No bother at all though there was a hairy moment when a patrol stopped us just beyond Clon, after we got the ammunition. The lad just threw it in the back but I got it pushed out o' sight before they saw it. Greedy bastards were more taken with our lobsters. Ah well I suppose we were lucky enough.'

He took a pull at his drink.

'Transfer in a barn behind the Munster Arms. Easy as pie.'

'An' the other?' asked Seamus.

'That too,' said Michaeleen, shaking his head. 'A sad business, Seamus. A dirty sad business.'

'Aye,' replied Heggerty. ''Tis so! 'Tis just so, but one that had to be done, friend or no friend. We all of us know the rules.'

Michaeleen shook his head again and stared into his drink.

'As you say, Seamus,' he sighed. 'As you say but God that Barry's a cool one. Never flinched. Thon eyes o' his! Aye well. Anyway 'tis their pigeon now, whether they like it or no. I'm not doin' it to a man I've known all me life. I just couldn't.'

He rubbed a hand across his eyes before looking up.

'That aside,' he said, 'we'll have to select the best men for the squad, but I want nobody married. Four along wi' himself an' me.'

Heggerty opened his mouth to speak but his friend stopped him.

'No, Seamus,' he said. 'Without tryin' to be smart, you're just past the middle years an' anyway, if the thing goes wrong, you'll be the only one left to carry on. Not a word Seamus. My mind's made up.'

They looked at each other without speaking. Then Michaeleen drained his drink.

'I'll see ye later when we've both had time to think. Only men we're a hundred percent sure of for I'm not goin' to be the one to ballacks this one up an' face yon boyo. There'd be no quarter wi' him,' he said, and, wiping his mouth with the palm of his hand, he went out into the pitch black evening, heading up the hill for the Castlehaven Road, one deeply depressed man, for all his successful delivery of the afternoon.

Eleven

Mick pushed open the front door.

'Is the tea ready, Mary?' he called down the hall. There was no answer.

'Are ye there, girl?' he called again. 'Get the tea on the table. I have things that need doin' before I get to the nets.'

He swung open the kitchen door and stood staring into the cold, empty room and the dead hearth. There was no tea, no Mary and no fire! He picked up the note propped against his tobacco jar on the mantelpiece and tapped it on his fingers without opening it. Then, stuffing it in his pocket, he whirled on his heel, left the house, slamming the heavy door behind him and strode along Cross Street before turning down the hill to the top of the village and banging the big iron knocker.

'Mick!' exclaimed Brendon's aunt in surprise. 'What's the matter? Is something wrong? Not the—?'

'Where is he, Annie? Where's that nephew o' yours? Is Mary with him? When did they go? The bastard! I'll shoot the whelp!'

The questions reverberated round the small cottage as he ranted, though he knew full well the answers.

'Hold on! Hold on, Mick!' cried Annie. 'Calm yerself. D'ye want a heart attack? Just calm down an' come away in ar that. No need for the whole village to hear yer business though mind they'll know soon enough in this place, and I'll remind ye, whatever else he is, he's no bastard.'

'When the hell did they go? Waited till I was away at the Market, the scutt!' he cried. 'Oh I knew they were plannin' it. She's been goin' on at it for weeks now but I paid it no mind. She threw it up at me the other mornin' even, the hussy.'

'Sit down, Mick,' said Annie. 'Sit down and calm yerself. Here, get that down ye,' and as she spoke she was handing him a stiff whiskey from a bottle on the dresser. 'Get that down ye.'

He drank it in one swallow and held out the glass which she recharged with, 'What are ye frettin' about anyway, Mick? Sure doesn't that leave the way clear! She an' Brendon are safely away out of it now so what is there to stop us?'

He looked up at her, the alcohol warming his stomach and soothing his ruffled feathers. She was a right handsome woman, still only in her thirties, and as the anger subsided, Mick's thoughts turned to companionable days and cosy evenings with a fine, warm wife waiting for him after a cold night on the sea.

'Hmm,' he mused. 'Ye may have a point there. I never quite faced that possibility. Hmm. What about Heggerty?'

'Oh he's more and more leaning to the Michael Collins camp,' she answered, deliberately misunderstanding his question. 'Sure ye already know that. D'ye want sausage? I have a nice bit of pig's kidney too.'

'Aye I know. I think Michaeleen's all right yet, though,' he answered, allowing himself to be diverted down that road. He finished his whiskey and refilled himself another.

'He still fancies ye, Annie. Ye know that,' he said reverting to his original question.

For answer, she tossed her thick fair hair and sniffed, deftly flipping over the eggs.

Sitting there quietly he sipped the drink and looked at her.

'Well if he's leanin' that way he'll find little sympathy around here. There's a fierce resentment in Cork County for Collins and his Treaty notions in spite of his past glories against the Brits. The most of us think we can totally defeat them this time. Heggerty's my Lieutenant an' you know what the Good Book says about a house divided, Annie. Collins is preachin' there'll have to be a Treaty. He says we can't defeat the whole British Empire.'

'Does he forget the Americans did?' she said dryly more from conversation than conviction, intent on her cooking.

'Aye but we haven't a Washington among us an' we're divided already. God, Annie, I'm gettin' I don't know who to trust but I'll tell ye this. Collins or no Collins, it's this time or never.'

'I wouldn't doubt that at all,' she answered, 'but what can we do? We mightn't have a Washington but as sure as eggs we have a Benedict Arnold.'

He looked up at her without understanding.

'Traitor, Mick. Traitor! We have that all right. We'll just have to watch our backs.'

For some minutes he was silent, working out the connection. Then it dawned and he laughed, 'Huh, once a schoolteacher, always a schoolteacher, Annie, eh? He was the bastard turned his coat from green to red? Aye well, it's Michaeleen, I'd be wary of. He's the deep one aye an' clever with it. Ye'll never know what he's thinkin'. We met a patrol this mornin' an' ye should have seen the way he handled them. Cool as a cucumber, Annie. Cool as a bloody cucumber.'

He sipped his drink, reflecting on the incident, then went on, 'Even out in the boat at night I can't get the whid of him.'

He helped himself to some more whiskey, staring down into the drink.

‘I tell ye, Annie, he’s not as slow as he walks easy that one. Heggerty’s up front about it and gives a body an argument, but not him. Cards close to the chest our Michaeleen.’

‘But why then did he save Brendon with the fish in the boxes?’ she asked, pouring out strong black tea.

‘Och,’ he said, ‘sure it’s obvious, Annie. All done to frame me. I was the only other one who knew the landin’ spot. It’s perfectly obvious. With me framed and court-martialled, who becomes the Commandant for the district? Mr Seamus Heggerty an’ his pal Mr Michaeleen Carey, my very own partner! Then they take the whole flyin’ squad an’ join Mister Michael Collins. Oh the plan’s plain as day to me, but I’ll have a say in it yet.’

‘Surely,’ agreed Annie, ‘but who do they turn to with their accusation, tell me that?’

‘Our friend from Cork of course. Who else in the county but Mr Thomas Barry and I can tell ye which side he’s on. The good Lord himself won’t save us if they convince that one I’m the informer. Every time I look into thon eyes—’

Annie turned away, tending to her pan.

‘This big action?’ she queried, casually changing the subject. ‘Have you to go?’

‘Of course I have to go,’ Mick replied. ‘Wouldn’t it look good for me to be sittin’ here and the rest away on operations. Heggerty’s too old. Well not old but he must be close to fifty. He’ll not be there.’

‘Oh ye can be sure he’ll not be there,’ she answered, a little wry smile playing about her lips. She turned from the range.

'Now come on, sit yerself down an' eat before it gets cold.'

She placed the fry on the table and rattled a knife and fork out of the drawer.

'Anyway, when and where is it to be? Who is it this time? Some County Court Judge or even the bold Joe Byrne himself, the RIC Inspector General. General Sir Joseph Aloysius himself would be the grand target, what?'

'Aye true for ye but he hasn't told us yet,' he replied, draining his glass and pulling up his chair to the table, 'but it's mighty big, Annie. Mighty big is all I know for sure. There's a man in Macroom Castle. That's all I know. We'll be told in good time,' and as he fell to eating, wondering if she knew that he was lying and why, she joined him with a mug of tea and stared thoughtfully across at the busy rugged face.

Twelve

It was strange that nobody noticed the influx of cousins, uncles and long-lost friends who straggled into the remote cottages between Macroom and Dunmanway towards the last week in November. Well it wasn't that nobody noticed, for of course they did, but that not a whid of it reached the Authorities, for one not in the know could so easily have dropped an innocent remark in shop or pub. At any rate, all the Volunteers from West Cork were billeted in and around Clogher by the twenty-first. During the following week, the thirty-six new lodgers had been visited by Mr Barry, resplendent in pink hunting jacket, doe-skin jodhpurs, shining leather boots and black bowler, to be briefed and forcefully instructed as to the repercussions if this were misadventured. As he passed the several Crown patrols, he would bid them a hearty time of the day and ask, 'Seen any foxes on your rounds, gentlemen?'

They saluted the Master of the Hunt, little knowing that they were looking at the wiliest of the species, for as he searched the countryside for a 'suitable site for the Christmas Hunt' he was surveying and eventually choosing his killing ground.

Mick and Michaeleen quietly supped stout from a case of bottles beside the big turf fire in a cottage on a little hill overlooking Gleann Chapel. They sat in silence, for the household were in bed and each was busy with his own thoughts. Suddenly there was a tap at the window and both men started, though this was what they had been waiting for since they had arrived separately after Mass on Sunday. Mick lifted the bar on the back door and, after a few brief muffled words, dropped it back into its hasps and came into the room with a long package, wrapped in oilskin.

'Slide them behind the dresser,' he said after unrolling the skin to reveal two pristine Lee-Enfield .303 rifles.

'Ammunition?' asked Michaeleen.

'In me pocket,' answered his companion. 'Tells me there's only thirty-five rounds apiece. Two wee boxes. In the porridge meal tub. Push them well down. It's hardly likely they'll be raidin' here but ye never can be sure.'

This done, the men resumed their seats and their silence.

After some time like this Mick said, 'Yer not much of a companion the night, Michaeleen.'

'I've a bad feelin' about it,' answered Michaeleen. 'Did he give ye the day?'

'Sunday comin',' replied his Commandant. 'The information from Macroom Castle is that the whole Intelligence Officers have been ordered to Cork City for a high level conference an' they set out on Sunday afternoon.'

'God, Mick, I have a bad feelin'. Sunday? Hardly a day for slaughter,' mused his companion.

'Ah don't be an oul' woman, Michaeleen,' his friend snapped. 'The sooner them bastards is got rid of, the sooner Ireland will be a nation once again. Government of her own. Freedom Michaeleen! Freedom for our children for generations. We're close Michaeleen. We daren't weaken now.'

His partner sighed and looked down at his hands, curled in his lap.

'Och yer right, yer right of course, Mick,' he answered, 'but I'd rather be haulin' a net wi' these than handlin' what's behind the dresser. It's clean out there beyond. Clean and fresh! Aye in fair or foul weather, Mick, 'tis cleaner than this an' a man can sleep easy in his bed.'

'Them days'll come back,' replied Mick. 'We mightn't see them after Sunday but they'll come. This operation is only a step, a big step, mind ye, but only one till they finally get the message, an' believe me, Michaeleen Carey, they will get the message this time.'

His companion pulled the cork from another bottle of stout in the crate and filled his tumbler gently with the hand of an expert. He sipped at the creamy froth, then drank deeply, staring into the fire.

'Aye Mick,' he mused as much to himself as the other, 'an' d'ye think many of us will know any difference? One master's much like another so far as I can see. From for ever, there's always them that drive the cart an' them that pull it.'

'Listen, Michaeleen,' answered Mick, 'there's more to it than that. There's principles involved here. There's freedom, freedom, Michaeleen!'

'Ah freedom me arse,' snapped his companion. 'D'ye know, Mick, I'm sick o' the word. Nobody ever interfered wi' me before all this started. I was free to come an' go as I pleased. I fished, ate, slept and none bothered me. Freedom? Freedom for what? Did ye ever think about it, Mick? What'll change for you an' me, aye an' the rest of the country? Just a different set o' clowns holdin' the reins!'

'You think too much, Michaeleen,' said Mick with a sigh, 'but whatever about that and Sunday's outcome, won't it give Collins a bit of pause for reflection? This is the only thing the Brits understand. A bloody nose an' a whean o' bodies sent home in bags'll make them readier to talk to him. The big stick, Michaeleen! The big stick is the only way. Partition will solve nothin'. 'Twud leave the country at each other's throats for a hundred years.'

His companion sipped, nodding.

'Oh I'm sure you're right there, Mick,' he said. 'I'm not afraid for myself for ye know I have nobody dependin' on me, but by the Lord Jesus, the revenge will be only mighty. They'll ravage the whole county. Mark my words. God help every Cork man and woman for their vengeance will be fearful an' I'm only wonderin' about the worth of it all.' He drained the tumbler in one long swallow and reached for another bottle.

'Yer a strange one, Michaeleen,' said Mick, following suit. 'You're my Lieutenant an' yer talkin' like a Father Confessor or a fool. Ye know it has to be done. I see what Collins is at but we have to keep up the pressure in the meantime or nothin'll get done. Treaties are got from strength, Michaeleen. From strength and this'll give us a mighty muscle, no matter the cost.'

In turn he took a pull at his pipe and his pint. They sat in silence till, with a change of emphasis, Mick remarked, 'Aye an' here, I hope ye have warm coverin' wi' ye for the courier's after tellin' me we have to be in the woods behind Kilmichael Cross, on Saturday. We're to be in place the night before the attack.'

'Oh it's Kilmichael, is it? Nice to know at last! So there'll be no Mass on Sunday then?' asked Michaeleen. 'No Mass save one with land after it, an acre!'

Mick looked puzzled for a moment and then smiled across at his companion's black humour.

'Massacre is a hard word, Michaeleen, but these are hard times. Sunday'll tell the tale. If yer feelin' that way, why not dander down an' see the priest the morra. I have the word he's one of us so there'd be no harm done. Nip down after dark why don't ye? Anyway, that's the message an' we've to be there all Saturday night. Now let's try to get some sleep. There'll be damn little in the next few days and for a while after that an' all.'

Michaeleen finished his drink and set his glass into the big Belfast jaw-tub under the window. He stared out into the misty moonlight, deep in thought for the attack was not the only thing he had on his mind. Then he turned away and went across to the sofa in the corner and lay down, face to the wall. Mick sat where he was, stretched out his legs to the fire and closed his eyes.

'Aye,' he thought, 'a queer one indeed. Wants me dead an' shys from killin' the English criminals that do be raping our country. Aye Michaeleen, yer a quare one an' of that there's no doubt. I'll be watchin' me back anyway, me proud bucko.'

He set down his empty glass on the tiled floor and drifted into a shallow doze there where he sat but Michaeleen lay listening to the rising wind moaning sadly around the old chimney, its mournful sough matching his own mood.

Thirteen

Coming into his uncle's kitchen, Brendon took Mary's hand.

'Have ye all ready, sweetheart?' he asked, kissing her upturned face.

'Aye all I have to get ready,' she replied, eyes sparkling with delight at their imminent departure. 'Sure I had only time for one wee case before he got back an' you collected me.'

She leaned up and kissed him.

'Oh Brendon, I can hardly wait,' she breathed. 'I can hardly believe we're actually on our way out of all this. You're sure it's not as bad in the North?'

'Hush, hush,' he said. 'Of course it's not. They're all Protestants up there, on the British side, so there's hardly any Tans about at all an' anyway we'll not even be there that long if you have yer way.'

He laughed down at her and pressed her close.

'We'll stop with my mother's folk outside Burton Port till we get organised.'

'Oh organised indeed,' she said smiling up at him. 'Is that the new name for it?'

He returned her smile.

'Och you know what I mean,' he answered. 'It'll take a wee while to organise the weddin'. If I remember right, old Father O'Byrne is a stickler for the rules. Ye know, the bans an' all that rubbish.'

'Oh Brendon,' she cried, laying her head against his shoulder. 'Oh Brendon, if anything happens this time I'll just die. Just die!'

'Don't you be worryin' your pretty head,' he said, kissing its curls. 'Nothing's going to happen this time. We'll be on the Cork train before ye know it. One night in Aunt Annie's friends' boardin'-house and then the Derry Packet Steamer an' goodbye to all this bloody nonsense. Then we're for Donegal, God's own country, and our own life.

'Now are ye ready? Johnny's bringin' round the gig shortly. He has to pick up a friend on the way too an' then he wants to drop us off in Bandon first. He an' his mate have some wee errand to do after. We have to be in Bandon for the Cork train by seven, so he's leavin' us off first. We'll be far too early but I'm sure we'll find somethin' to do with our time.' He gave an exaggerated wink as she gently slapped his grinning face.

'Oh I don't care about anything now, Brendon. We're on our way an' that's all that matters. I know it's only three now, but who cares. We're finally on our way,' and she hugged him tightly to her, before gathering up her meagre belongings as the rattle of the wheels stopped by the front door and Uncle Harry called, 'Come on you two or he'll be off without yis.'

He helped her up into the trap and handed her the small case.

'You take good care of this lovely girl, Brendy, or I'll come after ye with a twelve bore. Good luck to yis both. May God bless yis an' may the road rise wi' ye. Drop us a line now an' again.'

And with a crack of Johnny's whip, they were off to their new life.

Fourteen

The sun never parted the heavy lowering clouds that Sunday. By two o'clock, Barry had his three dozen men deployed on the rock-strewn, heather-clad slopes, either side of the narrow road. They were relieved to get their limbs stretched after the long cold wait of the previous night in the small coppice a hundred yards back. The slight mist had never quite risen and the men were constantly drying slippery hands, whether damp by the elements or cold sweat. Mick and Michaeleen lay on their heavy overcoats a few yards apart with McCarthy and Murphy on one side and O'Brien and a man from Bantry on the other.

'All set, men?' The soft voice behind startled them. Barry was making a final inspection of his Volunteers' disposition.

'Ye have more than an hour yet. Smoke if ye like. They'll be leavin' about half three but they'll not be here till around four. Good luck an' make every bullet count, for that's all we have.'

Michaeleen turned to look at him before he passed on. A shudder ran through him as he stared into the eyes of the man, now dressed in a British Army Officer's cap and tunic, Sam Browne belt over it and deep bottle-green riding trousers.

'Ye like it? Don't be shootin' me by mistake!' he smiled with a mock salute and in a moment was gone along the row of waiting men.

Michaeleen turned back to his rifle and the road curving between sloping banks, not twenty yards below him.

He lit a cigarette and threw the packet across to Mick.

‘It’s not the pipe,’ whispered the latter, ‘but it’ll have t’ do. Are ye all right?’

His Lieutenant nodded and drew smoke deep into his lungs. He thought of Heggerty, safe and replete after his roast chicken, warm before the fire in Annie’s kitchen, and no doubt thinking the same things as himself. They were quite convinced the informer was their leader but the whole thing was wrong. If that were the case, why was he here? Why had he not betrayed the plan to his English friends? Surely young Brendon couldn’t have been his only objective? Of course the exact date, time and position had been kept secret till yesterday but . . .

Michaeleen couldn’t figure it at all. Contact would have been difficult at that stage but they would know there was something on at least. His body shook a little. He wasn’t easy at all. He and Heggerty were sure, but if all else failed it was himself who would have to do it. Surely Mick hadn’t been willing to see his daughter’s fiancé captured just to have her as a housekeeper. That didn’t make sense, never mind the loss of two boxes of rifles. The Castlehaven one had only been fertiliser, but the Rosscarbery betrayal? That was something else.

Michaeleen’s head was in a whirl. As he thought he had grasped one solution, it slid away into the morass of another question or inconsistency, equally plausible, till, in turn, that one melted into the sand as well. He knew Headquarters in Cork City would have the name by now but no orders had been passed to him and here was that very traitor, if such he be, lying beside him, about to execute one of the most dastardly exploits in a long line of dastardly exploits on both sides.

‘The nature of Civil War,’ thought Michaeleen. ‘There’s never a clean one.’

Suddenly he stiffened. He tilted his head to listen. Horse's hooves! Definitely horse's hooves! He dragged the Albert from his pocket. Four o'clock already! God, where had the time gone? There was a movement on the far side of the road and in the gathering dusk, the figure of a British Officer stepped into the road, holding up a hand to the trap with three men and a girl, seated back to back.

'Halt,' called the officer in little more than a whisper.

Again Michaeleen's ears pricked up but this time it was the rumble of petrol engines approaching from the same direction.

'Get off the road,' hissed Barry for it was he who had stopped them. 'Get off the road, damn you. Up that track! Quick! I'll deal with you two later. Go! Go damn you!'

Mary and Brendon looked at Johnny and the man he had picked up and then at the uniformed officer before them. The lad started to protest but his driver slapped a restraining hand on his arm.

‘Shush, man! Don’t open yer mouth,’ and he wheeled right and galloped up a cow track into the copse. Scarcely had they cleared the way when a piercing whistle from the lookout, high on a rock away to the right, barely preceded the rumble of engines and the first of two Crossley Tenders rounded the bend behind them and slowed as the man in the middle of the road raised a hand again.

Even before the horse had slithered to a stop among the trees, without a word, Johnny and his friend grabbed two rifles from underneath the box-seat, jumped down and vanished back through the undergrowth, leaving the two young lovers staring speechlessly at each other.

Below them on the road, the squeal of brakes could be heard as the first vehicle came to a stop with another a few yards behind, almost colliding with it. Its driver stepped down and sauntered towards the uniformed figure, thirty feet ahead.

The surprise was utter and devastating!

Suddenly the silent gloom of the afternoon was shattered with the flash and roar of the heavy Smith and Wesson and, arms flailing, the man, chest blasted apart, hurtled backward crashing onto the wet road. Almost in the same instant, Barry, smoking .45 in left hand, hurled the Mills bomb with his right, with consummate accuracy into the one side of the windscreen. The explosion shattered the other side into smithereens, and with it the officer sitting there, leaving the Crossley totally blocking the narrow road, its cab a smoking ruin. Then like a mountain goat, he was up the bank and among the rocks calling,

‘Fire, lads! Fire! Leave none of the English bastards alive to tell the tale. Fire!’

And all hell erupted that Sunday afternoon on the quiet country road at Kilmichael as three dozen rifles and assorted small-arms, poured their death and venom into the two stationary Tenders of British Auxiliary Officers only yards below. In fewer minutes than it takes to tell, everyone in the first lorry was dead or wounded and the whole firepower was concentrated on the second. Suddenly from the rear one, a white handkerchief was being waved.

'Hold lads, hold!' cried Michaeleen. 'They're surrendering. Hold fire.'

The shooting died and finally spluttered to silence. Six figures struggled from the Crossley and emerged hands high, a white rag fluttering from one high-held hand. Michaeleen let out his breath which he seemed to have been holding for an eternity and lowered his rifle to the damp grass. He dropped his head onto the stock and made a silent prayer. It was over and he was still alive.

Then he actually screamed in disbelief. From the scrub behind him, although he hadn't known he was there, Barry and two others emerged and sprang down the bank, pausing a few yards away from the soldiers. With rapid rifle fire they coolly mowed down the surrendering men till only a pile of bloody black bodies darkened the road.

'McKelvy, Mitchell, O'Byrne,' Barry called, and with the three from the farther bank, he led them among the carnage, coolly putting revolvers to heads still breathing and pulling triggers till the lingering smell of cordite and an eerie silence fell over the Kilmichael countryside.

'Dead men can't identify,' he said, climbing back up the bank. 'Now away to yer lodgin's, gather yer stuff and be out of the district in the hour. Hang about at yer peril. Them that dies'll be the lucky ones. Michaeleen, pick up Mick's rifle. Dismissed.'

Stunned by the cool brutality, Michaeleen hardly heard him. He crawled across to Mick.

'Jesus, did ye see that?' he whispered. 'Christ I knew them eyes was killer's eyes. Come on, Mick. Let's get away from here double quick. There'll be a bad day ferneanst this. Come on.'

He began to creep away but there was no answering comment or movement.

'Jesus Mick, come on ar that,' he said, turning to urge his companion from the bloody scene. It was only when he peered closer into the twilight of that November afternoon that he saw that his Commandant was rolled over on his back and a large calibre hole oozed blood and brain from the middle of his forehead.

There was no need to check pulse or heartbeat. He lay gazing at the dark wound and the grey matter spreading down over the eye and cheek. He stared in dumb horror. That bullet hole? There was something not right here but his numbed mind refused to function and, with heaving stomach, he rose, turned away and vomited into the bushes. And in this, he was not alone.

'Pick up Mick's rifle and get to hell out of here,' snapped the voice behind him. 'Ye didn't think it was goin' to be a picnic, did ye? Ye can be sick later. This place'll be crawlin' wi' Auxies an' Tans within the hour. That shootin' will be heard for miles. Go, man, go!'

Wiping his mouth Michaeleen did as he was ordered and stumbled away from the road. A horse whinnied and he froze. Surely the mounted patrol could not be here already. He parted some whin bushes and there, Brendon holding the bucking horse's head, stood the trap, Mary clinging on inside for dear life.

‘Mary,’ ‘he exclaimed, emerging, two rifles trailing. ‘Mary! Brendon! Holy Mother o’ God, what are you two doin’ here? Where the hell did you come from? I thought you were away North.’

‘Michaeleen!’ she breathed. ‘Mr Carey. What—?’

She broke off as Johnny and his friend pushed past.

‘Get down quick, Mary,’ said the former, dragging a body to the rear of the trap and hoisting it in with as much reverence as could be managed in such an operation.

Mary stared down at the bloodless face and the large oozing hole in the forehead.

‘Oh Christ, no!’ she screamed and fainted into Brendon’s arms, oblivious to the rest.

Seconds later, Barry emerged through the bushes.

‘Get O’Sullivan in there too. I’m not leavin’ him to be mutilated by the bastards. Gently with Deasy. He might live yet. Now you two,’ he snapped, turning to Johnny and his friend, ‘get this trap away to hell from here to the doctor in the Dunmanway safe house. Off with ye. Take the turf track round Annahalla Bog. Go!’

‘You,’ he said, wheeling on Brendon. ‘I dunno what the hell yer doin’ here but I’d advise you, young man, to get your girlfriend as far away from Kilmichael as your legs will carry you and if there’s one word escapes, I’ll know who to come for. Move!’ He turned back to the scene of his carnage.

‘Get to your uncle’s,’ hissed Johnny over his shoulder, whipping up the horse. ‘Keep to the fiel’s. It’s yer only chance. They’ll not stop to ask questions after this an’ they’ll not spare Marry either. It’ll be dark in no time. Hurry lad! Ye haven’t a second te lose.’

Brendon, heart pounding, knelt beside Mary, gently slapping her cheeks, with tears of incredulity running down his own, for this brought his escapades fully into focus. This was no game now. This was no exciting adventure. This was bloody horror itself.

In minutes the dark men in caps had melted away from that slaughter and, over field, sheep-track and bog-road, gained their temporary lodgings. Rifles were hastily buried in thatch, hayloft or manure-heap and belongings gathered. Indeed before that hour had passed most of them were quite gone, heading through bracken and gorse over the wild Cork countryside for their respective homes.

'Hurry up, Ryan,' urged one such to his friend as the woman of the house scuttled around them, terrified to be sure nothing of their presence was left.

'I'm nearly right, Eamon,' replied his companion. 'Don't fuss, man. They'll never have mustered out yet! We've piles o' time.'

The farmer entered, breathless after his efforts.

'The guns is safe for the present but I want them outa here. Them bastards'll take the place apart. They'll not lave one farm within five miles of Kilmichael Cross. We'll be lucky if we're not all burned to the groun'.'

'Don't worry, Sean,' answered Ryan. 'They'll be collected before the week's out. We'll have need of them again, ye know. This is not the end.'

He shouldered his knapsack.

'Ready, Eamon?'

Suddenly the four froze. Outside there was a step on the cobbles.

'Jesus Mary an' Joseph! Hissed the woman. 'Mother o' God save us. They're here already!'

There was a battering at the door.

'Into the room,' whispered the farmer. 'The big cupboard by the chimney.'

The two snatched their packs and disappeared, closing the bedroom door behind them.

The battering was repeated.

'Open up for the love of God,' came the English voice.

'Comin',' answered the owner and lifted the wooden bar from its hasps, allowing the door to burst open.

'Help me,' cried the officer, falling half into the kitchen. 'Help me, missus. Ambush! They've nearly done for me. Thought I was dead.'

Bridgett bent over the blood-spattered soldier and looked enquiringly up at her husband with ashen face, but before he could speak, the two lodgers had rushed from the room, thrust her roughly aside and dragged the wounded man by the feet back into the yard. Without the least hesitation, one of them pulled the man's revolver from its holster and put two bullets into the back of his head.

'We're off,' said Ryan, pocketing the weapon and nodding at the bloody corpse. 'Get a neighbour and dump that in Annahalla Bog. It's bottomless. It'll never be found there.'

Without another word, they shouldered their knapsacks and trotted away across the cobbled yard and out onto the moor into the gathering night.

Fifteen

The old Coastguard residence was a hive of oil lamps, hard-boiled eggs, thick home-cooked ham sandwiches and strong sweet tea and stout, with other personal beverages arriving in inside pockets or hip flasks according to personal preference. Neighbours came and went, offering their condolences to the stricken young girl, her hopes and dreams in ruins with her father lying stiff and cold below in the room. How they had got the body home she neither knew nor cared. Suffice to say that Father Burk and Uncle Harry had some hand in it and he had been buried without IRA honours as the victim of a massive heart attack, certified by Doctor Cross.

Indeed how they had got home themselves she hardly knew. She could remember lying that freezing night in some barn or other with Brendon holding her tight under the warm hay, and where Johnny and the trap had come from the next morning she neither knew nor cared. Everything was just a haze of memory till they found themselves climbing off the train in Skibbereen. Deasy had not survived his wounds and Jim O'Sullivan had died on the spot, making a total of three of their men dead and the county was being ravaged under Martial Law.

Heggerty and Michaeleen sat alone in the parlour by the coffin.

'They've burnt Kilmichael, Inchageela and Johnstown. Burnt to the ground. Jesus God.'

'Aye,' said the publican 'and I hear friend Barry took some sort of turn. Annie heard he was in Cork Hospital.'

'I'll shed no tears for that gent,' replied Michaeleen. 'I knew what would happen. What about the three poor boys they beat to death in Bandon Main Street. God what a shambles and us not let out of our houses after nine o'clock wi' Tans on every corner, struttin' an' bullyinn' even the children. Thon eyes of his. No more feelin' than a rat.'

'Aye,' said Heggerty. 'True for ye, Michaeleen. True for ye.'

He took a flat bottle from his coat pocket and stiffly laced the mugs of tea.

'Put a bit o' backbone into it,' he said, slapping the cork back into the flask with the heel of his hand. 'An' we'll need it for a few months yet I'll warrant.'

They sipped his tea in silence but each knew what the other was thinking. At last Heggerty said quietly, staring down at the tea held between his knees, 'Saves us a dirty job though. I couldn't a done it.'

Michaeleen's thoughts returned to the man lying dead on the bank at Kilmichael. He had pushed the horrors of that afternoon as far from his consciousness as possible, considering how recent it was, but as he sat there, the picture forced itself back into his mind's eye in every gory detail and suddenly it hit him. With a trembling hand he raised the mug to his lips and drained it.

'Barry!' he whispered.

He had come from the bushes behind to leap down the bank and finish off the surrendering soldiers. From behind and that gaping hole in Mick's forehead and the small one at the back! It was as clear as day. Orders from Headquarters in Cork City and Mr Barry planned it to perfection with the British to blame for local consumption. Oh yes, Mr Thomas Barry knew precisely what he was doing. Aye.

'Pick up Mick's rifle,' he had said!

Thereby hung the whole truth. How had he known? There was only one answer. Another noble martyr for dear old Ireland and that was that. God he wouldn't be surprised if they didn't make a song about him.

'What's the matter?' asked Heggerty, staring at his companion whose face was pale even in the yellow oil lamps. 'You look like yer goin' to be sick.'

'Aye ye might just say that, Seamus. Ye might just say that. That Irishmen have come to this! May the good God forgive us!'

'Well,' mused Heggerty, 'The job's done anyway. That's one good thing came out of it.'

'What good thing?'

They looked up at Annie, standing there quietly in the doorway, holding a plate of sandwiches. 'What good?'

'Well,' answered Michaeleen after some thought, 'this place is Mary's now. Nothin' to stop her an' Brendon marryin' an' stayin' right here. No need for them to, well, get away from things now. Surely there's some good in that? This village can't afford to lose it's young folk, and with Mick gone, we'll see they're not involved any more.'

Annie was silent but as Michaeleen stared into his empty mug, her eyes found the publican's and a fondness passed between them.

'Hmmm,' she said. 'Aye but ye see, this place is never hers. Mick, God rest him, never got the papers signed.'

All three were silent.

'Well damn me,' said Michaeleen at last. 'He always gave me to believe it was his.'

'Well it isn't an' ye can be sure the Crown will want to sell it now as vacant premises so there mightn't be all that good come out of it after all.'

The men nodded, taking her point.

'Anyway, you'll have another cup an' a sandwich? You, Seamus? There's some nice ham an' cheese! I'll get more tea.'

Without waiting for an answer, she set down her plate and left as quietly as she had come and Michaeleen wondered just how long she had been standing there before she spoke.

Though they daren't have held a proper wake, which would have lasted till dawn, it was well past curfew when the last mourner slipped quietly from the back door and made his way over the fields to his home. Annie and Mary started to clear the debris of dishes while Brendon and Heggerty sat quietly on either side of the fire, deep in thought.

After some minutes, as if by common consent, their heads raised and their eyes met and each was quite certain that he knew what the other was thinking.

Heggerty lowered his gaze and stared into the smouldering turf.

'A bad business,' he said quietly under the rattle of dried cutlery being thrown into drawers. 'A damn bad business.'

Brendon nodded, answering, 'Aye a damn bad business as ye say, Mr Heggerty, the whole bloody parcel, wrappin' an' all.'

Behind the clatter of dishes Heggerty answered softly, 'Bury it with Mick, lad. Bury it now with himself this very night. Let it lie there with himself an' his good name.'

With a deep sigh, Brendon nodded his assent and tried to close his eyes and a chapter of his life.

'I'll walk ye down, Annie,' said the publican. 'We'll take the back track. They'll be on the road an' they don't stop to ask questions these days.'

She looked over her shoulder from the big stone jaw-tub and nodded while her nephew watched, deep in thought.

'I'll just sit here, Mary,' he said. 'I'm not leavin' ye alone on this night. We have things to talk about anyway.'

After the older folk had slipped out into the darkness and Mary was still busy tidying, Brendon walked to the window and stared down at the sea far below, listening to its distant roar, just audible from beyond the village. His mind was back in the pub as Heggerty laid the trap for the informer. Only the Army Council and himself knew his destination and significantly one of those was now dead. The lad was no fool either for he had noted the hole in the back of Mick's head as it was hoisted into the trap. If the Commandant was the rat, there was absolutely no doubt that Mary must never know and continue to believe that her father died for Ireland, nobly in action.

But what if he were not? As much as Brendon detested the man, yet he couldn't believe it was he, now conveniently dead and unable to defend himself. That left four, any of whom it could be if he could unravel it. His mind went back to the couple of incidents when he had been almost killed, for he was in no doubt that, had he been caught with the stuff, he must surely have perished unceremoniously on Rosscarbery Pier from an English bullet, lovingly delivered.

Just the four left. He would stake his life on Michaeleen and Heggerty. He simply couldn't credit either as an informer. Not Michaeleen who had virtually saved him that first night. No, it couldn't be Michaeleen nor Heggerty with his fondness for his aunt. What was he thinking of? If it were, why would they have swapped his boxes from the freighter? Then he turned his mind to who might be the other men on the Army Council. He knew there were two others, but who were they?

Oh God it was a mess. His mind couldn't cope but there was one thing for sure. This time he was finished. No more! He had made his last run no matter who ordered him. He and Mary were going through with their plans and nobody was going to prevent it. Mr Heggerty was right. He must and would bury the whole dirty business with the man they would lay in his grave on the morrow and leave it and him six feet under the Castlehaven sod.

He felt her arms go around him from behind and she, crying softly, laid her head against his back.

'Oh Brendon, Brendon,' she sobbed and he turned and held her tight, then led her to the sofa.

'There now, my Mary, he's gone but like many a true man before him, he died for Ireland. He's in good company now.'

'Died for Ireland?' she almost screamed, green eyes flashing in the firelight. 'Died for Ireland? A great pity they couldn't live for Ireland instead. The English will go. Our Michael Collins will see to that somehow. They will Brendon. They'll go without all this slaughter. It'll take time but they'll go without all this killing. Look what Kilmichael has done to the county. Burnings, lootings, murders and mayhem across the countryside and my father lying cold in the front room there. He loved me, you know, Brendon. He loved me for all his hard ways. Never lifted a hand to me in his life! He never got over mother's death and I was all he had left of her. Never!'

She began to weep again and he put an arm round her shoulder and rocked her gently.

'I know, I know,' he said. 'I know he loved you and most of his anger at me was his thought of losing you. I know, my Mary. I know.'

'All this and not a step nearer so-called freedom,' she cried. 'I am free. I don't give a damn for their politics. What difference will it make to us? We'll have the same life anyway. Oh Brendon, take me away from this bloody country. Ireland be damned if this is the price we have to pay. Take me away,' and she fell sobbing into the cushions. He stroked her hair gently and knew that for all his strength, he was going to find it hard to stick to his resolve never to let it slip but just as surely that he must. He eased her into his arms and cradled her there till she fell into an exhausted sleep.

Sixteen

Early in the new month, the Tans burned down the centre of Cork City, which atrocity seemed to assuage their vengeance somewhat, but as the dark days of December crawled inexorably toward the Festive Season, everybody knew it would be a bleak one in the county and the rest of Munster.

Some shops in Skibbereen strung coloured streamers of twisted crepe in their windows in a vain attempt to conjure up a hint of the spirit of festivity and fat turkeys and geese hung in McCarthy's butcher's shop. In Baby Hanna's pub on Bridge Street, conversation was muted around the big fire and ceased completely when a five-man patrol would throw open the door, plant a grenade on the counter, demand drink which was hastily provided without the benefit of payment to the establishment and, pints in hand, stand with their backs to the bar, daring any customer even to raise his head, never mind speak.

Going about their business, men and women kept their eyes averted, lest a look would be taken as open defiance or dumb insolence, two handy phrases for the bully. People spoke in whispers, glancing over their shoulders from time to time and even the children had ceased their boisterous anticipation of Santa Claus and presents.

The Tans took the middle of the street when patrolling, all carts and those few motor vehicles slowly crawling behind them in silent fury till they decided to stand aside to let them pass, smirking with satisfaction at their own intimidating power. Up and down the county houses were raided, many burned down, seemingly for the love of it and well dare anyone offer even a verbal objection to the bullying and open thefts from retail premises.

The officers, cigarettes dangling from mouths, stood idly by, while one or other of their men would enter a shop, pick up a shirt from the rail, carefully fold it up, drop a brown penny on the counter and leave with it under his arm. Fear and resentment were almost palpable among the locals but none dared speak and the Constabulary, an RIC Sergeant and four men, no doubt knowing their limitations, kept themselves conveniently somewhere else on other important duties.

'They were bad before,' remarked Michaeleen in Heggerty's, 'but they're brutes now, thanks to Mr Barry's kind of war. I hear they sacked Balbriggan above Dublin there, nearly burning it to the ground but for the intervention by a few hundred Police from camp on the Curragh. That's what Barry's methods have brought on us. Holy Mother, is not the white flag of surrender accepted in any conflict throughout the world? Oh maybe not among some of them African savages ye read about but we're supposed to be civilised. Even the British have some sort o' religion, I hear.'

'How is he anyway?' asked the publican.

'I think he's out of hospital but I'm told he'll never be right. The heart, I am told,' answered his companion.

'Ah well, it's all the bastard deserves from what ye tell me. Thon's no way for men to fight a war. Where's the difference between that an' the Tans' brutalities?' replied the publican. 'Thank God we're stood down till the New Year.'

He sipped his eleven o'clock tea for he had a rule about drinking behind his own counter. '1921,' he mused. 'God wouldn't ye wonder what it'll bring?'

'It couldn't bring worse anyway,' replied Michaeleen. 'It couldn't bring worse. The word is we're to carry on with our normal lives till we get orders from above. I fancy that'll be a good few months off yet wi' them rampagin' across the country. Aye an' wi' the light nights comin' on, 'tis better to leave it for the present.'

He was silent, searching for his pouch.

'How's Annie?' he asked as he sliced tobacco, rubbing it in hard hands and filling his pipe.

'Oh fine,' Seamus answered. 'Just fine but she's a bit worried about the nephew. Mary's takin' the father's death hard. He wants to stay in Ireland but she's mad to get away altogether. She's for America but he's content to stay where he is on the home farm an' take up the fishin' again in Donegal.'

'Donegal, eh? Ye don't happen to know where?' mused Michaeleen, watching his friend's face closely.

'Oh somewhere near Burtonport, I think,' answered Heggerty. 'I wasn't all that interested but they're better away from here anyway. Lucky enough they were to get out again, after their last attempt. Could ye believe it?

'Annie wouldn't hear of him bein' used again but she needn't have worried. He came to me shortly after the funeral and demanded that I clear the way with the County Commandant. Said he wasn't to be hunted as a traitor the rest of his life. He's well known to the authorities now and better watched.

'Tell ye the truth, we'll be contenter with the pair of them gone. There's nothin' here for her either now. The order from the Coastguard Authority ordering her to quit the Station arrived a few days after Mick died. Sensitive bastards, whatever they want it for. Jeeze ye could see a platoon o' Tans in there yet.'

'Aw Seamus,' said Michaeleen, 'don't even joke about it.'

'God knows what's goin' to happen with Mr Collins an' the Treaty talks,' said his friend, changing the subject. 'I'd be for it if only to get a bit of normality back and them Tans away to hell from about us.'

'Aye,' sighed Michaeleen non-committally, striking a match and applying it to his pipe. 'There is that.'

He drew smoke into his mouth, pressing down the swelling tobacco with a tough, practised forefinger, stared into his pint, sipped and set it heavily down on the table.

'Annie an' you, Seamus? ' he asked.

'I dunno,' replied his friend. 'I dunno. She talks about marryin' but there's somethin' stickin' in me craw. I can't just pin it down but it's there all the same. Some wee niggle I have when I let meself think over the incidents of the gun-runnnin'. I dunno. I just can't get a handle on it at all. Some way it's too pat. Oh she's a fine woman an' I have a deep affection for her but, well, sometimes there's the odd word. Och I dunno, Michaeleen. Maybe I'm an oul' bachelor too stayed in me ways for marriage.'

'Och it's just the times we're in, Seamus,' answered his friend. 'We're all livin' on our nerves. It'll pass when things quieten down. They can't keep this up for ever an' then you'll feel different.'

'Aye maybe,' said Heggerty, draining his cup and staring into the tea leaves like a fortune teller. 'Maybe so, Michaeleen. Maybe so.'

Seventeen

He was right. 1921 passed quietly in Munster. Oh there were still individual atrocities and murders up the country, mainly in South Armagh and Wicklow, but along the Cork coast men and women settled back to the fishing or weaving or tending their small farms, albeit under the vengeful eye of the Auxies and Tans, while the illegal Parliament of 1919 tightened its grip on the country and more and more the King's writ did not run.

In fact, many sympathetic civil servants deferred to De Valera and his Sinn Finn mandate of seventy-three seats. Lloyd George formulated a plan for Ulster to be coerced into an all-Ireland Republic in the arrogant hope that familiarity would ease their fevered objections to being ruled by a Roman Catholic State, but Bonar Law, not to mention the Northern Unionists under Carson, soon put an end to that line of thought, with the Ulster Volunteer Force of 1912 vintage beginning again to make ominous rumblings as well.

Castletownshend's leisurely progress through the first years of the third decade of the twentieth century passed for normal but Michaeleen and his friend knew full well that it was a lull before an internecine storm, for the Treaty talks were going on apace and those opposed were beginning to make their objections felt, up and down the country.

De Valera had cleverly prevailed on Michael Collins and Arthur Griffith to negotiate with the Welsh Wizard, himself keeping out of it till finally, in December of '21, the Treaty was signed, with the North Eastern Six Counties excluded on a promise to review that border later.

Full of misgivings, for he was nobody's fool, Collins returned and immediately left the capital to seek solace in the company of her who would provide it, one Miss Kiernan.

They sat together, her head nestling on his shoulder, one cold dark afternoon in the upstairs parlour of her father's Hotel in Granard before a roaring turf fire flickering its warm, yellow light on the baubles adorning the Christmas tree in the corner.

'You an' I know 'tis the best we could do at this time, sweetheart but I tell you, Kitty, my love,' he confided, 'I have just signed my own death warrant.'

She tossed her dark hair and laughed.

'Nonsense, Michael darlin',' she scoffed. 'You're the saviour of your country. The rest will come later. We'll unite in time. Are not three green fields better than none?'

'Ah Kitty,' he answered, 'I know that and you know that but there's them across the country that have the name o' traitor on me already. There's them that'll never accept the twenty-six. Even our friend Arthur is beginning to distance himself an' he signed the damn thing alongside me. Sure didn't I feel it on the boat comin' back. He was far too damned quiet. Every time I opened the conversation, all he would say was, "Lave it, Michael. Lave it alone will ye? I'm sick o' talking about it. Just lave it lie. Let history decide."'

She snuggled into his shoulder and drew her legs up under her, kicking off her shoes.

'Let's forget it, darlin',' she whispered into his hear. 'Let's enjoy these few days we have together for all too soon you'll be away again about your Master's business.'

She laughed and he kissed her.

'Master indeed! I wonder,' he said. 'I hope he's a friend as well for I've the notion on me that I'll need all o' them I can get.'

He turned and took her in his arms and there, in that flickering warmth, the silence and the evening closed in around them, as the first few flakes of snow began to slant across the window.

Kitty's prediction proved so right for, early in January of the next year, 1922, the cumbersome manoeuvrings of replacing one administration with another began. Among the rest, the withdrawal of the Tans and their Cohorts was celebrated throughout the land. This unmourned collection of professionals, convicts and bullies left Irish soil finally in March and, almost a year to the day after the Treaty had been signed, the Irish Free State, with Dominion Status, actually came into existence on the sixth of December, 1922.

During this time Kitty's fiancé's duties were of necessity so numerous and involved that she hardly saw him, though the newspapers kept her abreast of his progress. In that summer, Collins, the founder some four years earlier of the Irish Republican Army with its Flying Squads of young killers of British personnel, had appointed himself the Commanding General of its legitimate fighting men in July and began a countrywide tour of inspection to rally support for the Treaty. Griffith, soon to shuffle off the mortal coil, had finally disassociated himself from his friend's 'betrayal' and had deserted him publicly.

'Now who's the traitor?' thought Kitty when she read it. 'They don't know the giant of a man they have.'

Thus the Civil War, formerly a smouldering ember for years against a common enemy, burst into violent conflagration up and down the land with brother against brother, father against son, and all against their former enemies, including the ex-Policemen who, if truth were told, kept the brutalities of the Black and Tans to a minimum, as far as was in their power.

The conflict spilled over into the southern counties of the new Northern Ireland State, whence many of the disbanded RIC had sought sanctuary, joining the newly formed Royal Ulster Constabulary and thus finding themselves back in the middle of it once more with bomb and bullet their daily companions.

Eighteen

The back room in the out-of-the-way bar in Mitchelstown had only the two occupants for the barman had locked the door. The dark-haired man, white-winged at the temples, well-dressed in business suit, fly-away collar and red tie, peered through his steel-rimmed spectacles, sipped his drink and looked across the table.

'I don't know exactly but you'll hear. He's makin' no secret of it. Says he's certain nobody in his own county will harm him. Can ye do it without attachin' blame? I suspect with one thing and another, it'll be in August sometime, for I happen to know he has several commitments before that.'

'You get me the date, sir,' said the man opposite, 'and I'll guarantee a result. Oh I have a few men I can still trust.'

'You'll have no bother with the date,' answered the man, taking off his spectacles and polishing them with his breast-pocket handkerchief. 'He'll make sure the whole county knows he's coming.'

'Back to God's own country,' he keeps sayin'. Oh you'll have no bother knowin' the date.'

His companion lifted his pint and nodded.

'Just you leave everything to me, sir.'

The other took out a packet of cigarettes, proffered it across and lit both with one of the new petrol lighters. He leaned back in his chair, blew smoke to the ceiling and swirled the brandy in his glass.

'I'm told you still have a wee bit of internal trouble down in your part of the country,' he said, studying the end of his cigarette. 'I thought that had resolved itself at Kilmichael eighteen months ago?'

'Don't worry, sir,' replied his companion. 'We still have some dissenters but I am having that taken care of. No, no, you have no worries there. I'll see it doesn't interfere with the business in hand.'

'Good, good!' said his companion, rising and adding thoughtfully, almost to himself. 'Sadly, it has to be. Aye it has to be.'

He stubbed out the cigarette, picked up his briefcase and soft hat and said, 'Well I'll be off back to the hub of activity. Someone has to keep a watching brief for with all these disbanded RIC men roamin' the country, anything could happen and I want to keep a lid on that for we have all we can handle at the minute. Good day to you and good luck.'

He tapped on the panel to be let out and two thick-necked heavy-set men dropped their newspapers and sprang up from their chairs at his appearance and fell in behind him as he made for the rear entrance and a long black Daimler sitting in the yard.

The roar of its engine had scarcely died away before the door reopened and a small grey-faced man entered, sat down on the still-warm chair opposite the occupant, removed his hat, grimy and green with a red cock-pheasant feather sticking from the black band, and, setting down the pint he held, leaned his elbows on the table with, 'Well, Master, is it on?'

Nineteen

Meantime the Christmas of 1922 had come and gone and although the British had left completely a few months afterwards, it was memorable only for its close resemblance to its predecessor and its absence of the Festive Spirit as the people began to rebuild their shattered lives and their ransacked homes. The New Year was into its fifth month, with the sixth anniversary of the Easter Rising only a couple of weeks past and rumblings of discontent with the Treaty gathering a pace throughout the length and breadth of Ireland. Mary and Brendon were gone back to Uncle Harry's on the first step of her secret dreams and the county was returning to an uneasy normality. The curfew imposed after the slaughter at Kilmichael had gone of course, though in those days few were abroad after dark anyway. The ravaging of the county after these two bestial incidents seemed to have satiated the blood lust on both sides, and then the Treaty had been signed the previous December. For the moment then, the most southerly Province of the island found some respite, at least so far as the uninvolved citizen was concerned.

There were, however, not many cheery waves and shouted salutations for Seamus as he made his way along the main street, turning down the entry into the supplier's huge yard, surrounded by warehouses, in the back road in Clonakilty that beautiful May morning. Oh everybody knew him, knew him well, but though things had quietened down, the normal banter and good nature of the Corkonian was still waiting in the wings for Mr Collins' efforts to bear fruit, with a good few who wished that the fruit would be a rotten apple and were poised to squash it under foot.

Across the cobbled yard, the large, red corrugated iron door beneath 'W J McQuade, Wholesale Wines and Spirits' in bold, chipped white lettering was half open.

‘’Mornin’, John,’ called Seamus as he entered and made his way through roof-high rows of firkins, hogsheads and cases of bottles to the small, grimy-windowed cubicle at the rear, constructed of flattened cardboard boxes nailed to a few four-by-twos attached to floor and rafter.

‘Ah Seamus, me bucko,’ answered the big ruddy-faced man in shirt sleeves held back by blue elastic bands, soft hat planted on the back of his shining head. He was scribbling with an actual goose quill pen into a large book covering the most of his ancient, Dickensian desk. ‘Top o’ the mornin’ te ye. An’ isn’t that a grand one to be alive?’

‘It is that, John,’ replied the publican. ‘It is that. Keepin’ well?’

‘Can’t complain, Seamus,’ answered the supplier. ‘Can’t complain. Same order as last month or is there a bit more consumption since things have quietened down with the departure of our friends the Tans?’

Seamus shook his head, looked around him, along the aisles of liquor and lowered his voice.

‘Is it all right?’

‘Safe as the confessional, bucko,’ answered John. ‘Safe as the grave.’

Leaning back, he took a couple of cigarettes from a packet propped against the large inkwell, stuck one in his mouth to replace the but he was grinding out in the huge Guinness ashtray and passed the other across to his guest.

‘Well?’

With another glance around, the publican asked, ‘Is he comin’?’

‘He’s comin’,’ answered the supplier. ‘He’s comin’, God save us! Down to see the family and review his loyal followers an’ old comrades.’

The two men looked at each other and both sighed.

'Jeeze doesn't he know there's them that's just waitin' for the chance?' said Seamus. 'I hear snippets in the pub when the tongues get loose wi' the stout an' believe me he'll be treadin' on dangerous ground, no matter what he thinks of his old mates.'

John nodded in silent agreement and his friend went on, 'Would there be any persuadin' of him?'

'None,' was the reply. 'Absolutely none. "If I can't go home in my own country," he says, "then the whole piece isn't worth the full o' me arse of boiled snow." So he's comin' an' wild horses'll not change him.'

The supplier had produced a bottle of whiskey and two shot glasses from his desk drawer and was filling them with a practised hand.

'To himself, then,' he said. 'May the Good Lord keep a weather eye on his back,' and both men touched glasses before draining them in one.

'Well I'll try to give the Good Lord a bit of a hand if I can, some way or other,' said Seamus as a refill was set in front of him.

'A bird never flew on one wing bucko,' said John as he slid the glass across.

'Yer health an' his. I have a couple I can trust an' we'll keep our ears open an' I'll set up some sort of protection, though there's not a great deal I can do if he's intent on his walkabouts.'

He sipped at his drink this time.

'I'll be close by anyway an' I have a wee notion just who I might need to be lookin' out for. No names, no pack drill, but I've heard whispers an' I can tell ye it's a bit of a revelation when I think of the same non-entity.'

Both men were silent, contemplating their drinks.

'I dunno, John,' continued Seamus then. 'I've a bad feelin' in me water about it. Why the hell doesn't he stay where he is. If he's killed in my section, we'll be the lepers for a hundred years. The county that murdered Collins! Huh! Some epitaph.'

'End of August,' John said. 'Ye have a few months yet.'

'Aye a few months,' mused Seamus. 'If only I could get whid of their plan. Hmm. I'll dwell on it, I will.'

John rose from his high chair.

'Anyway I know you'll do what ye can to see he's safe. Will Michaeleen be on side?'

The Castletownshend publican hesitated fractionally, rubbing a toe of his boot on the dusty floor.

'I think so, John. He's a fair man, a thinkin' man,' he answered. 'I think so but in these times, who knows anybody's leanin's? I'm not a hundred percent. I'll have to give that one a deal of thought between this and the end of August. A good deal of thought though I do know he was mightily concerned over the final brutality at Kilmichael.'

He set his order on the ledger, drained his glass and buttoned his jacket.

'It all needs a damn good deal of thought,' he said. 'See you next month, John, an' if ye hear anythin' in the meantime, you'll let me know. Good luck,' and he made his way back down the rows of high-piled barrels to the entrance and headed in the bright sunshine for the main street.

John stared after him for some minutes, then shook his head and returned to his books, lighting another cigarette from the last one. He looked longingly at the bottle of whiskey and then yielded to a small splash before replacing it in its drawer.

Then and only then did the slight figure edge from behind the wine cases, stacked to the roof against the rickety office, smile crookedly to himself, slip quietly out of the trap in the rear of the warehouse and, skirting the drays lined up in the yard, make his way up an entry and into the back door of an adjoining pub, where the grey-faced man in the grimy cock-feathered hat sat staring into his pint.

The small grizzled yard-man slipped onto the stool beside him.

'I'll try a pint as well,' he said.

Twenty

It was a beautiful July night, warm and starlit. The apple blossom had given way to pippins and the summer had been good to the farmer, with its soft rain and long days of sunshine to swell the grain and grow the grass.

It was close to midnight. The last of his customers had gone and Heggerty had shuttered the big window and now stood on his front step, staring up the street at the yellow light in Annie's cottage window. When young Kelly had brought the message, he had washed, shaved a second time, and put on his new green tweed jacket and a collar and tie. He had a fair notion what the conversation would be about for it was well over a year now since Mick had died and they had been accepted by the village as a couple. He still wasn't sure what he was going to say but now that things were almost back to normal, maybe a wedding wasn't such a bad idea, never mind the extra help in the bar.

He would give it a wee while yet to let the neighbours get to sleep but minutes later the curtain obliterated the light for a few seconds and then the movement was repeated a couple more times.

'Huh,' he muttered. 'Anxious! She must have somethin' on her mind.'

He straightened his tie, buttoned his jacket, pulled the pub door behind him, squared his shoulders, and with, 'Don't be gettin' impatient now, Annie, dear,' started up the steep hill.

Outside the door he paused, ran a hand over his hair and a finger round his collar to ease its unaccustomed restriction, and, lifting the latch, pushed it open and entered the dark hall.

'Annie,' he called softly. 'Are ye there, girl?'

Two flashes and two shots shattered the night. Without another sound, the publican fell forward, half into the kitchen, never knowing what hit him.

In the chair, bound hand and foot, Annie screamed.

'You said you were only going to talk to him!' she shouted. 'You promised. You promised. Oh God in Heaven, what have I done? You promised. Talk, you said. Only to talk!'

'I lied,' said the man without emotion, 'a technique you're fairly familiar with, my dear lady.'

She began to weep uncontrollably, slumped forward in her bonds, wild eyes staring at the prone figure on the tiles at her feet. This wasn't how it was meant to be. This wasn't the noble struggle for independence. This wasn't why she had tried in her own way to avoid the mindless brutalities and preserve some sort of sanity around her beloved village. This was just bloody internecine murder, the very thing she had been endeavouring to prevent. The Tans were one thing but this . . . this was Seamus . . . this was the man who thought as much if not more of Ireland than the rat who had just murdered him.

'Oh God!' she moaned. 'Oh dear sweet Jesus, is this what we've come down to?'

'That's one of yis,' he said, looking at the body and ignoring her outburst. 'Now they're all my men.'

He emphasised the 'my', and paused, still looking down at the bleeding body. Replacing the revolver in his coat, he stood reflecting for a moment.

'Hmm,' he mused without any show of emotion. 'Hmm. Maybe there's just one more. Hmm. We'll just have to wait and see. At least that settles your wee plans as guardian angel, talkin' to me in yer bar, as if I was trash.'

He stepped over the body, looked up and down the deserted street. No light showed. Nobody rushed out to investigate the shattering of their sleep. Men held their breath and lay still in their beds.

He closed the front door.

'An' you have a care, Mr Michael Collins, when ye dare to put a foot in Clonakilty, trumpetin' yer feckin Treaty and Partition. We're not restin' till we have it all an' be damned to ye,' he said, going back into the kitchen and looking down at her as he tied a drying cloth across her mouth, with another to blindfold her. Then his eyes narrowed and he put his stubbled face very close to hers.

'You'll be all right, Annie, trussed up like that, but mind: one stray word and we know where Burton Port is an' the Donegal men don't shirk their duty like some I could mention. Good night to ye, ma'am.'

In the next moment he was gone by the back door, the red cock-pheasant's feather in his hat, brushing the transom as he stepped out into the night.

'One unit, one aim, one Commandant,' he said softly as he climbed the hill. When he stopped and paused for breath he took a long look up at the old Coastguard house, empty now and staring blind-eyed out to sea over the roofs of the sleeping village.

'No room for appeasers or informers, eh Mick? No room, Mick. It's all or nothin' this time.'

Moving aside into the tree shadows around Admiral Somerville's estate gates, he looked up at the big house for a long time, shook his head thoughtfully, and drew out the heavy revolver and replaced the two rounds he had just fired, carefully dropping the empty cases into the pocket of his long coat. Then, pulling the old hat down over his brow, he started along the Castlehaven Road where a mile away, through the trees, he could just make out, high on the bluff above Sandy Cove, the oil lamp in Michaeleen's window.

It was Mrs Rafferty, calling for fresh eggs next morning, who rapped and then pushed open the door. She stood aghast for half a minute, let out a wild scream and, raising the village with her wailing, ran for the Sergeant.

Annie just sat there silently, tied hand and foot to the chair with gag and blindfold still in place. She was calmer now for she had had the whole night to think, there with the stiffening body of a man she would have married. Now her mind was finally made up. She had been dubiously selective before. Now she knew she was right. These men, the vicious ones, must be stopped or they would surely plunge Ireland further into an internecine conflict of Irishman against Irishman, which would never be resolved.

God knew how many more Kilmichaels there would be. That one had only claimed three but the British had taken a terrible vengeance for their dozen and a half butchered comrades. This would be ten times worse when it got properly started. She knew it wouldn't stop with one or two. Something would have to be done, for as sure as rain, a civil conflict with neighbour killing neighbour would put the Brits and their atrocities into the shade. The country would tear itself apart. Compromise had been found. Surely time itself would take care of the rest.

'Oh Seamus, Seamus,' she sobbed behind the gag, 'how many more good men must die like dogs before it's over?'

'I don't suppose you know who it was?' the Sergeant asked as he took off the blindfold and untied her.

She shook her head between her sobs.

'Never saw him. Came in the back door. I was sittin' here in the firelight, waitin' for Seamus. Oh God, my poor Seamus. Mother o' God. Oh Seamus, Seamus.'

'No,' replied the Policeman thoughtfully. 'Somehow I didn't think ye would, Annie. I didn't think ye would. Nobody ever sees or hears anythin' these days. The whole country's suddenly gone blind and deaf!'

He stood up from the cold corpse and spoke to a lad among the onlookers.

'Hop on yer bike, Barry, and tell the Sergeant in Skib. He'll know what to do. Here's sixpence. Away wi' ye now,' and he flicked the coin to the boy who caught it deftly and was off like a hare.

Twenty-one

Every man in the village attended the funeral as Father Burk committed the publican to the ground in what in effect would become the last grave in the old cemetery in the plot beside his erstwhile commander, Mick. Michaeleen stood in the warm summer sunshine, looking down the slipway of the small inlet on a full tide, from the sparkling blue wavelets breaking gently against the surrounding rocks, to the stony beach and soft green fields along the narrow Rineen Peninsula on the other side. This was the peace he longed for throughout his Ireland and not the brutal savagery which had brought him there. God when would it end!

He turned his head and surveyed the gathering of dark-suited mourners, scattered in twos and threes between the graves. Across the black, gaping, clean-cut rectangle in the earth, Monaghan stood, old hat for once not on his head but held reverently across his chest. Their eyes met, held for a brief moment and moved away. Annie, in grey jacket and skirt with matching hat, covered her face in her handkerchief, silently weeping as the coffin was lowered at her feet. Heggerty had no living relatives and it was common currency that he had left the pub to her long since, though that was far from her mind just then. Michaeleen's eyes rose from her bent head and over to the gate where the two men stood under the trees on the other side of the lane. They wore light shower-proof, belted coats and soft hats, well pulled down. They had arrived in a long black car after the service had begun, parked at the end of the small slipway, sauntered up and taken position opposite the entrance. Michaeleen watched as they seemed to carefully scan the assembled villagers, till their eyes spotted Monaghan by the graveside and lingered before moving on. The priest intoned the final prayers.

'For as much as we brought nothing into this world, so just as surely we can take nothing out . . .'

He bent to pick up a handful of rich dark earth and continued, dribbling it onto the coffin lid, 'Ashes to ashes, dust to dust.' He looked around his assembly.

'Now let us pray for the soul of our dear departed friend, a fine honourable man, laid low by a murderer's bullet. Our Father which art in Heaven . . . ,' and like the poor Timothy Winters, Monaghan's voice could be clearly heard above the rest, uttering the loudest 'Amen. Aaaamen.'

With the first shovelful of crumbling earth rattling hollowly down on the coffin lid, Annie turned away, Brendon on one side and Mary on the other, making their way slowly across the old graveyard. As he followed their progress over the mounds of long-forgotten resting places, Michaeleen's heart missed a beat for, in that same flicker of time, he saw the fleeting glance of recognition that passed between her and the two men outside as she made her way out to the patient pony and waiting trap.

'It was so good of you to come, Mary, dear,' she said when they were settled on the red leather seat. 'It's an awful long journey but I'm so glad you made it. You too, Brendon, of course. I couldn't have got through these awful days without you.'

The girl was silent as he cracked the silver-butted whip over the pony's ears and they set off at a trot up the old lane to the Coast Road where they wheeled right for the village and the Parish Hall, where the refreshments awaited the mourners.

'It changes things,' was all Brendon said, and Mary winced through her tears. She knew it would and that knowledge gave her no pleasure at all. She knew the work involved in running a village pub and the hours it would take, just as she surely knew that was going to be her and her husband's future in Castletownshend. It was goodbye to America and all her dreams which had so excited her as they stood hand in hand at the altar in the little chapel by the lake in the beautiful glen at the headwaters of the Gweebarra River, in the heart of the Donegal mountains, surrounded by Brendon's relatives and friends.

She thought of his grandfather's cottage like a picture on a chocolate box with its canopy of red and yellow roses and its neat thatch which was to be their home after their honeymoon in the Hotel in Bundoran. That alone had started to weaken her resolve for the New World but now she knew that it was all irrelevant anyway. This was her future for Brendon couldn't leave his aunt, whom he loved and who had been so good to him after his mother had passed away, to run the bar alone, even if he thought she could. Mary knew in her heart that there was nothing she could do about it. She sighed deeply and rested her head against her young husband's shoulder as they reached the village and turned up Cross Street for the last tribute to Annie's dear friend and a man who would be sorely missed in the village.

Twenty-two

It was only weeks later and the streets of Skibbereen were lined two and three deep as ecstatic crowds craned their necks to see the visitor. Mothers held up their children so that they could tell their offspring that they had seen the great Michael Collins, Ireland's freedom fighter who, with his will-o'-the-wisp Flying Squads had brought the mighty British Empire to its knees, or at least dented its confidence that it was the undisputed ruler of almost half the world, civilised or not.

The hood of the long Ford was thrown open and he stood up in the back, hat held high to right and left as the three-car motorcade made its circuit of the little town, finally turning up North Street towards Leap. There too and next in Rosscarbery, the cars slowed to a crawl as the residents left their kitchens, bars and shops to get a glimpse of the mighty man as he progressed to his birthplace in Sam's Cross at Woodfield, just outside Clonakilty.

He leaned forward and tapped his driver on the shoulder.

'The next road on the left, Pat,' he said.

''Deed I know it well, sir,' replied the other over his shoulder. 'Have I not rabbited these fields for years as a lad? Oh I know it well, sir, but 'tis a sad sight now, more's the pity.'

'Have ye been back since?' asked the man sitting beside him in the back.

'No, Liam! I have not,' replied Michael. 'I have not an' to tell ye the truth, I'm sort o' dreadin' it. We moved into that house when I was ten an' it still holds grand memories for me.'

He was silent, eyes and thoughts far away, clambering walls and leaping streams with fishing rod or snare, Patch barking ahead, enough to scare any rabbit or trout clear out of the parish. Then he shook his head and said, 'Still, Liam, me boy, that's all in the past now. If there's any more burnin' an' brutality, we have only ourselves to blame. England was a handy punch-bag, aye, an' deservedly so, but now we're on our own if Himself would only come right out an' back the Treaty. If he doesn't, I'm afraid we haven't seen the half of it yet.'

That and all, his sister, Maggie, had decided that the only place literally to hold his reception was on their land at the site of the home where he had been reared and spent the happiest years of his youth before going off to London to work for the Royal Mail. They had cleared away the blackened rubble left after Captain Percival and his men had visited their gentle justice on the new house only months before with sprinkled petrol and a match while her mother and sisters looked on in stony-faced silence. They had been driven out with bayonet and rifle butt and had watched from the hillside, shivering in the cold early April night, till neighbours led them away to shelter and warmth.

Many willing hands had spread cartloads of gravel over the charred remains, while nearby the children delightedly fuelled the great tea boiler with what was left of rafter and door frame. Their mothers had set up tables, groaning with many contributions of roast lamb, pork, fish and sliced soda farls spread thickly with yellow country butter, under the three great oaks which had watched the Tans and their oft-practised destruction.

She had the whole family assembled and with the countless well-wishers from near and far filling the yard, for it was a glorious August day, there wouldn't be much of it left. Somehow everyone was served with cups of the strong brew and sandwiches of their choice and within an hour her prophecy had been fulfilled, the dogs quarrelling over the remaining bones.

His speech was stentorian but brief for he knew he must press on in spite of the chiding of his Colonel beside him.

'Friends, thank you for coming. Thank you most sincerely. I think Maggie and all you good ladies must have cleared your cupboards with the spread ye put up. Feedin' the five thousand wouldn't be in it, aye, an' me due for lunch in Bandon in a couple of hours. I'll have to loosen me belt.

'I'll have to be goin' now friends but I promise ye I'll be back to raise again me old home on this very spot. That has to be the attitude. Put it all in the past and rebuild Ireland as its people want it, not at the behest of others. Good luck to yis all an' thanks again. It gives me great heart to see so many of yes bothered to come and say hello.'

They cheered themselves hoarse till he lifted a hand.

'And, like Mister Dickens's Tiny Tim said, God bless us, every one,' and so he began to take his leave.

With Maggie linked on his arm and Liam close behind, he squeezed among the throng, shaking welcoming hands with a word for those he knew and a smile and a pat on the shoulder for those he did not, till finally he reached the small wrought-iron gateway in the dry stone ditch giving onto the lane and turned.

'There's one man's hand I want to shake before I go,' he said, scanning the scores of smiling faces before him. 'I believe James Santry's son is here. Where are ye, lad?'

A powerfully built young redheaded man easily pushed his way through the throng.

'I'm Jim Santry, sir,' he said and the hand that Michael took could have crushed a coconut.

'It's my great pleasure and privilege to meet you Jim,' said Collins warmly, extracting his bruised fingers. 'I used to hang on every word your father said, there twenty-five years ago in his forge. He and his stories of our brave patriots had a good part in makin' me what I am today, whatever that is.'

Another mighty cheer rang out from the spectators, echoing away down the valley below. He smiled and raised a hand.

'I just lived for his tales of the Bold Fenian Men of his day as I pumped the bellows in time to the ring of hammer on anvil. D'ye know, Jim, I imagine even now I can still smell the lovely tang of burnin' hoof as he clamped the red hot shoe to it, makin' smoke rise to the rafters.'

Behind her hand, his sister smiled, for so could she as Jim's only suit of heavy blue serge, barely containing the bulging muscles, even in chapel retained that lingering odour of smithy smoke which permeated the whole place from his labours in the forge that was now his own livelihood.

'I'll have to be off now, Sis,' he said, giving her a bear's hug. 'You'll be able to get to the weddin'? Kitty wants you all there. We're havin' it in her father's Hotel, you know, the Greville Arms in Granard.'

He laughed.

'You'll find it easy, for come to think of it, 'tis the only Hotel in Granard,' and he laughed again. 'You'll be there?'

'Try to beat me away,' she laughed. 'We'll all be there, Mick. Do you think we'd let our famous brother steal away quiet like? Sure the crack'll be only mighty.'

'Ah that's great,' he said, giving her another hug. 'I'll see there's cars for yis all at Ballywillan Halt. Get to Mullingar, then to Longford and they'll put ye on the spur to the wee station, if ye could call it a station. The cars'll be there waitin'. I'll post ye the date. 'Twudent be the same without the whole of yis there.'

She stood on tip-toes and kissed his handsome face, a shadow passing over her bright eyes for a fleeting second but disappearing as quickly as it had come.

'You take care now. Hear?' she said.

'Oh stop fussin', Sis,' he laughed, hugging her to him. 'Weren't ye ever the worrier? Don't you be listenin' to idle gossip. This is my county. All pigswill that talk, Sis. See ye at the weddin'.' And easing his way through the throng outside the gate, he climbed into the back seat, waving over his shoulder as they headed down the lane to the main road and turned left for the town, not half a dozen miles away.

'Are we goin' on through, sir?' asked the officer at his side, much more in hope than expectation. 'We should try to be back in Dublin before dark an' it's a brave stretch. Better than a hundred an' eighty miles.'

'Oh stop fussin, Liam,' answered Collins, patting his companion's arm and settling back in the soft leather. 'Sure it's daylight till eleven o'clock. You worry too much. You'll die young with it. Relax man.'

The uniformed officer, a man about his own age, sighed deeply and continued scanning the road ahead, eyes darting from one side of the road to the other.

Clonakilty was even worse than Skibbereen. There couldn't have been a single absentee from the fit population, young and old, who wasn't out, on pavement and windowsill, tree branch and even roof-top. They cheered their favourite son till they were hoarse and swelled into the main street so that even if Collins' aide had wanted, there was no way they were going on without stopping. A path was forged for him to the front door of Donovan's Hotel where he, hopping onto a barrel outside, turned to the massed crowds.

'My friends, thank you for coming out in such numbers. Believe me I am flattered beyond my limited powers to express. Thank you from the bottom of my heart. As long as I live I'll remember this day. Bear with me a few minutes more for I have only one thing to say to you.

'Let us now bury our differences, put the past behind us and make Ireland truly a Land of Saints and Scholars, with the odd jarvie and farmer of course thrown in and make sure that our future generations will be proud to bear the name of Irish.'

The crowd roared their approval till he raised both hands.

'I'll have a pint of Rassler,' he cried 'and a pint of the same for every man or woman that wants it.'

Another cheer rang out and must have been heard in the next town, sixteen miles away, while frothing tankards of the dark brew were filled by the three, sweating barmen and passed throughout the smiling horde.

'Here's to Mick,' shouted a leading citizen, 'the only man fit to stand alongside Dan O'Connell. Liberators the pair of them an' ours forby, a true Cork man.'

Another roar went up and they downed their drinks and W J McQuade's ferret-faced yard man drank and cheered as heartily as any man there.

It is not recorded just how many pints were distributed throughout that afternoon but enough pounds were stuffed into the hotelier's hand to ensure he made a fine profit on the day's business, before the party finally extricated themselves and headed for the next town.

In Bandon Liam was aware that the crowds, though numerous, were not so thick as to prevent the cars pulling along the main street and down the entry into the yard behind the Munster Arms, where a lunch with some local dignitaries including the priest and headmaster of the National School had been prepared. The former said Grace and for an hour they relaxed, passing themselves at nibbling the salmon and baked potatoes. Many rose to sing Collins' praises and toasts were drunk to his successes. Then the schoolmaster rose and with moving eloquence dwelt at some length on the brilliance of Collins in making the Treaty with Lloyd George.

'It's not perfect,' he concluded, 'but it'll have to do till we can get a better one. That day will come, Michael. Believe me, that day will undoubtedly come.'

It was over. Liam urged, 'Come on, sir. Times getting' on an' it's no great road from here to Cork. We'd better be away.'

Michael patted his shoulder.

'Boys, Liam, but aren't you the worrier,' he said. 'Still I suppose yer right.'

He gripped the hands of his hosts in turn.

'Goodbye, Father. Goodbye, Master Lyons. Goodbye to yis all. See ye soon,' and with a cheery wave he followed his aide to the waiting cars.

Twenty-three

Collins climbed into the front seat beside the driver.

'I want to see my lovely county, the biggest and most beautiful in Ireland, aye an' with the warmest-hearted people from Mizzen Head to Malin,' he explained. 'You lie back there and have a nap, Liam. It's a beautiful run along the river into Innishannon and Cork City. It could be a long time before I can see it again. We'll go in front. Francy an' Colum, fall in behind us,' and the three black cars moved slowly out of the little town by the side of the peaceful Bandon River winding its way lazily to the sea along its tree-lined valley, stretching away to their left in the afternoon sun, their sharp shadows undulating over the low banks alongside.

In a couple of miles, the river, on its way to the Atlantic, passed under the road which, curving up steeply to the right, began to enter a gap in the long ridge of wooded hillside. Suddenly on rounding a bend, a loaded hay-float and struggling horse totally blocked the way and Michael's driver squealed so abruptly to a stop that the two cars behind almost collided into each other.

Collins opened the passenger door and stepped out.

'Keep her at it, boyo. We're in no hurry,' he called up and the farmer raised his whip in acknowledgement but did not look back as he shouted his straining animal to greater efforts.

Collins turned to survey the peaceful scene of shallow water rippling over smooth, black stones below.

'One last look!' he said to his friend through the car window. 'Just one last look!'

It was exactly that. At the same moment, the sharp crack of a rifle from high up on the right, among the thick beeches, shattered the bright afternoon and the General's head. Michael Collins, freedom-fighter, Treaty signatory and Irish Patriot Extraordinary, was dead at the age of thirty-two, a single bullet putting a violent end to a violent life and all the promise for a changing future for Ireland. Almost before he hit the ground, Liam was at his side, kneeling, revolver in hand but only a gesture at that range, even if he could identify a target. Dropping the weapon, he lifted the bloody head from the dust and raised tear-filled eyes to the ridge and the road ahead and, wonder of wonders, the horse and its load had suddenly found wings to their efforts and were disappearing round the next bend.

Men tumbled from the cars behind, casting this way and that. Three headed towards where the faint trace of smoke still lingered over the hillside as the driver, born and bred not a mile away, helped Liam with the body.

'Bel na Mblath,' he whispered to himself. 'The mouth of flowers. A good place to die. The mouth of flowers!'

'Ah Michael, Michael,' cried Liam, cradling the bloody head from the dirt. 'I told ye. I told ye but ye wouldn't listen. O, Mother o' God didn't I warn ye a hundred times. Oh Jesus Mary,' and he began to sob openly like a child.

The three bodyguards were soon straggling back with the fourth returning from watching the haystack on its float disappearing down a lane a quarter mile away.

'Nothin',' said the first. 'Nothin' up there but an empty shell case and a few cock pheasant's feathers,' and he held out his hand to show both before throwing them to the ground.

'An' our bird has flown,' said the second. 'God knows where he is by now. Wastin' our time! 'Twud take an army to find him in that country.'

'Ah well,' said the third, 'it was always on the cards. Always on the cards!'

Grim-faced with eyes narrowing, barely controlling his rage at their seeming indifference, Liam glanced sideways at them as he and his driver eased the body along the back seat and tucked a car rug under the smashed head.

'Is that all ye can say?' he asked softly, gently closing the eyelids. 'Not much of an epitaph for the greatest Irishman you'll ever know. The bastard who did this wouldn't be fit to wipe his boots,' and he stared steadily at the men.

The four looked at him in silence, then, dropping their eyes, turned and shuffled back to their vehicles without another word.

'Not fit to scrape his boots,' he said after them, adding silently, 'just like you bunch of useless bastards and by the Lord Jesus I'll be givin' yis a deal more attention when we get back to Dublin.'

In Cork City, somehow the news had preceded them and the expectant crowds bared their heads in silent tribute and women openly wept as the cortège made its slow progress through the sombre streets on that bright August afternoon which was to unleash another violent chapter in Ireland's troubled history.

Twenty-four

The pub was empty but for the two of us. I sipped my drink as I waited, enthralled, pen poised over the last few pages of my notebook for the final instalment.

Castletownshend! I had known its name from my reading and research of 'The Irish R.M.' stories, and had driven down into the small village, just to have a look, en passant as it were, on my round-Ireland trip in the summer holidays, away from school, from increasingly unmanageable, disobedient children whose parents now thought that begetting made them teachers, and from the incessant bombings and murders of the poor benighted North. I hadn't the slightest intention of staying for longer than the observation would take and here I was, almost a fortnight later, still there.

I had turned from the little harbour with its quay and slipway and the estuary full of boats of all sizes and yachts whose pennants identified many nationalities, thinking that the large warehouse overlooking it would have made a grand hotel. I had decided that a light lunch here would save me having to stop later on, so with this in mind and needing nothing more than a sandwich and a beer, I passed Mary Anne's with its menu-boards outside and pulled in at the local bar, halfway up the steep street to get just that.

There I had found him as now, sitting alone with his Guinness and the day's newspaper folded on the bench beside him. I nodded and commented on the fine spell of weather we were having and asked if the pub did sandwiches.

'Not normally,' came the voice as a very pretty girl emerged from the door behind me. 'We really don't have the facilities for caterin' but sure we can't be lettin' ye away hungry. I'll certainly make you some. Sure amn't I doin' nothin' else!'

She went behind the counter, pulled my pint and said, 'Ham all right? Home-cooked this mornin' by yours truly.'

'Perfect,' I replied smiling and, returning it readily to show white even teeth, she went back into what I presumed was their living quarters.

I leaned on the bar and turned to face the old man.

'Are all the Cork girls as pretty as she?' I asked, looking after her at the closed door.

''Deed 'tis true for ye,' he answered, 'an' ye should see her mother, aye, an' grandmother forby.'

I think that was how the talk started, but at any rate I soon realised I had stumbled on the makings of a first-hand tale and a Homer more than willing to tell it.

As with our other conversations, I had waited till the bar was deserted before re-opening his saga. Now it was thus, silent save for the dripping tap and the squeak of drying cloth on glass as the lovely, dark-haired young girl polished tumblers, holding them up to the summer sunlight coming through the window, to check her work.

Twenty-five

'Well?' I prompted at last, reluctantly taking my eyes from her and jerking my narrator back to the subject in hand.

'Och that's about the whole of it around here,' the old man said, sighing wearily. 'The Tans were gone and the Royal Irish Constabulary disbanded. This left a gap filled by the IRA, struttin' around in their trench coats, revolvers strapped around their waists. But they were soon replaced by the Garda Síochána, thank God. Things gradually calmed down here though the Civil War still raged farther North into Wicklow and around Dublin an' on up to Louth an' South Armagh.'

He set his tankard down on the well-worn table and seemed to study it while he drifted again into the past.

'The lads stopped bringin' in the guns along this coast. With the Royal Navy frigates sallyin' out of Cobh or Queenstown as was then, for they still kept a few ports, ye know, it wasn't worth the candle. Och sure hadn't they enough arms anyway. Wi' the Treaty signed an' Collins himself shot at thon wee gap outside Bandon in August of that very same year, the Civil War took hold then about right. There was more Irish blood spilled in that than ever the Tans did. Sure Dev, when he took over, had his own best man executed as a traitor to the state!'

This time he looked pointedly at the empty tumbler in front of him and I nodded to the barmaid.

'Two more Mary and make mine a half,' I said, to which he hastily added:

'An' a shmall one to bore a hole in it for me.'

We smiled at each other, as I handed her the money before turning back to him.

'But that isn't all,' I protested. 'You can't just leave the story like that. Who was the informer? Who was the traitor? It surely wasn't the publican? Did Annie marry? Was she—? What about Michaeleen? Did Monaghan–?'

I was actually spluttering out my questions, anxious to rekindle his interest so that my story would have a conclusion, when he held up a hand to give me pause. He drained the whiskey in one smooth draught, tapped the last drops into his stout and took a sip.

'All a matter of history young man,' he answered. 'All a matter of history or private thought.'

'No! No! That won't do,' I said. 'You can't leave me hangin' like that. I've been two weeks compiling my notes on all you've told me up till now but I need a conclusion, an end. You're not going to leave me to make it up are you? You know so much you must surely know the rest?'

He took another drink and scratched his grey-stubbled chin with the edge of the glass.

'Well,' he said, 'I suppose there's somethin' in what you say. The young folk came back and the life was a deal better than the girl thought it would be. She an' Annie ran the house an' Mary was the best-loved landlady in West Cork. Her young husband took up the fishin' in earnest after buyin' back his beloved *Northern Star* an' made a good livin' at the salmon an' lobsters till the lorries stopped comin' the whole cut through Leap round here.

'They started loadin' the catches across the way in Rineen, Union Hall or Glandore, though 'tis all done in Union Hall nowadays. Still he an' his wife had a grand life an' when Annie died an' left her the pub, they ran it together.

Visitors would come back year after year, many of them buyin' holiday houses, an' damn the foot they would put in any other bar but hers. She knew everybody an' had a cheery word and a welcomin' smile for them all, never mind the wee favours she did in the village, unbeknownced to anyone. Oh nobody went without a pound or a few loaves, if she heard of it.

'They had one son. He an' his wife run it now. That's their daughter.'

He nodded his head at the young girl, now busy replenishing bottles of stout, wiping the neck of each before setting it neatly in its row along the shelves.

'The Coastguard house is long gone. The priest's is built where it stood. You pass it at the head of the village, above Cross Street, just there where the Grotto is.'

He sipped again and the old eyes faded back into the past once more.

'Monaghan and Michaeleen?' I prompted.

'Monaghan,' he mused, returning to the present. 'Nobody knows for sure what eventually happened to that boyo, aye an' few about here give a damn, either. It was put out that he went to America; others said Australia.'

He paused contemplating me across the table, as if wondering whether to go on or not. Then, making up his mind about something, he did continue.

'Neither America nor Australia ever felt the foot of him for I happen to know, never mind how, that he was shot in a low lodgin' house not far from Kilrush in County Clare. I don't talk much about that but ah sure who would listen to an oul' fool like me anyway?'

Again he stared steadily at me and maybe it was my imagination but I was sure the corners of his mouth were just about to turn up into a smile, but in the same instant it passed.

'A Volunteer settlin' some old score or other no doubt an' dumping him in the Shannon Estuary.'

Then a smile did crease his face and the old eyes twinkled.

'There's a wile strong current in the river there where they have the electricity turbines now an' maybe he did reach America after all.'

He chuckled softly to himself for some minutes till it brought on a fit of coughing. I waited till he had composed himself once more, wiping his mouth with his handkerchief and settling back in his corner.

'That an all, he was seen about Bandon when Collins was murdered an' was still comin' in here a dozen or so years later, when Admiral Somerville, that estate up at the corner there, was shot.'

He sipped his drink.

'Did ye know that he was the same family as the Somerville of Somerville an' Ross, them that wrote *Tales of an Irish R.M.*?'

I had known this and also that Siegfried Sassoon had stayed there for some months after leaving the Edinburgh Hospital, but I didn't admit it and feigned appropriate surprise at his information.

'Indeed?' I said. 'Very interesting. I've read and enjoyed it. Hmm. And they lived in that estate up at the corner? That'll be something to tell my class.'

I digested this for some minutes, suitably impressed, then got back to my purpose.

'So you think Monaghan might have been involved?'

'Well,' he said with a sigh, 'it came out that he was their hit man as they call it today in the pictures. He shot poor Heggerty down like a dog, so you decide for yerself. At any rate he was never seen around here after the Admiral was murdered. America? Australia? Huh! Meself, well I've told ye what I believe an' if anybody did, he deserved a good killin'.'

He held up the whiskey glass to the young girl and nodded at my tumbler.

'Michaeleen ran the local Flyin' Squad for a month or two but when Collins was murdered outside Bandon there on the twenty-second of August 1922, that was the finish. He had had enough of Monaghan's ways, decidin' to change loyalties and ended up a Major in the Irish Army, fightin' for the new Free State against the diehards, them that wanted all or nothin'.'

He lifted his pipe from where it lay beside the ashtray and lit the remains, puffing blue smoke into the sunbeam and watching as it floated up to add its stain to the dark rafters over our heads.

'And,' I urged after it was drawing well, 'what happened to him?'

He leaned back and puffed contentedly for some moments.

Like pulling hen's teeth, I thought, as I waited.

The old face hardened.

'What happened to Michaeleen? Well one day when he was home on leave and Brendon an' him were lyin' dryin' in the sun after takin' a swim at Tragumna round the coast road there – lovely wee spot. Have ye been round? Good pub, the Skibbereen Eagle, there if ye fancy a dropeen.

'Anyway, there the two o' them lay at peace wi' the world till a rifle bullet from among the rocks on the headland put paid to his military career. Some dirty bastard! Oh don't talk to me about the Law. Huh! The Gardi hardly formed an' most o' them sympathisers to one side or other. Routine inquiries an' that was the end of it!'

There was another long pause while he drew in smoke.

'They got him to hospital but the bullet was lodged in his lungs. No dacent surgery in them days.'

The pipe glowed once more. Then, taking it from his mouth and looking directly at me, he paused with the tumbler halfway to his lips considering some thought which seemed to have just occurred to him across the years.

'Aye an' come to think of it, Monaghan was still about then an' all! Hmm. God an' d'ye know, young man, 'tis the first time I ever put the two things together. Monaghan, be god!'

'Aye a likely story,' I thought, but refrained from comment, keeping a smile from my face with some difficulty.

His eyes held mine steadily for some moments. Then he shook his head, sighed deeply, and, lowering his gaze, went on, 'Hmm. Still around he was!'

I was beginning to sort this out in my head, fitting facts together with theories but he started to talk again, not to me but as to a long-lost friend.

''Twas the times that were in it, Michaeleen. The times that were in it an' the bad taste they left, aye to this very day.'

He stopped again and I thought I saw a single tear glisten in the pale eye but he rubbed one brown hand down his face and it was gone.

'Aye Michaeleen,' he went on, 'he's dead about, och it must be fifty years since. He was a fine man, an honourable man he was, an' d'ye know, that glance an' missed heartbeat in the graveyard at poor Seamus's interment beyond in Castlehaven never passed his lips. He an' young Brendon became good friends over the years but never a word was passed about it. He was visited by Annie as he lay mortally wounded from that fecker's bullet in the wee cottage hospital in Skibbereen in thirty-two.'

'I'd like to have been a fly on the wall at that conversation,' I commented.

'Aye,' he laughed, 'so would I but she would never talk about it, the more young Brendy tried her. Went to the grave with her a'n' him, it did.'

We sipped our drinks in silence as if in reverend memory of the incident.

'Aye a better man niver wore shoe leather! He knew full well what had to be done but he knew too there was right ways an' wrong ways o' doin' it. Even bloody wars must have some fecken rules or we're no better than them heathen savages.'

The silence was longer this time till I spoke.

'And Barry?' I asked, scribbling away. 'Whatever happened to Mr Thomas Barry?'

'Och ye can read all about him. Heart attack or a stroke or some such. Ended up in a nerve clinic, I believe,' answered the old man, tapping his glass on the table for he had been ignored by the girl.

'They've wrote books about that one. Aye books an' erected a monument to his ambush. Did ye go to see it? It's on the side o' the road up there at Dus-a-Bharraigh, Kilmichael. Take a run over to Macroom before ye go home an' ye'll pass it on yer right hand. 'Tis worth seein'. There's a relief map too in stone wi' all the positions of his men, lookouts an' all, set out wi' wee bulbs that light up whiles at night. It'll give ye the whole plan for yer book. The headstones to the three Volunteers who died are there as well. Aye well worth goin' to see. Och sure what am I talkin' about. Sure Mary'll show you where it is. It'll make a nice run for yis some evenin'.'

I nodded my agreement and made a note to make the trip with that lovely girl, for we had become closer than customer and barmaid by then – a great deal closer!

'He was only twenty-three, ye know,' he went on. 'I never met him but some make him out a butcher an' some a hero. I suppose it all depends which side ye were on.'

I digested this before asking,

'You haven't answered the real question, sir.'

I watched his face closely before continuing.

'Aye an' what would that be?' he asked, staring back at me.

'You had a traitor in your midst! Who was it? The traitor? Who was the rat at the malt? Was it really Mick?' I asked, for I could see a few shades of doubt about that conclusion.

He leaned back and his eyes never left mine. There was another long silence while he contemplated me and my question and I couldn't keep the hen's teeth simile from returning to my mind.

Then a tired smile added to the lines on his weathered face.

'Traitor?' he mused. 'Traitor? Just how would ye define a traitor? Has the word only one meanin', the dirty one? Did ye ever think about that an' you a schoolteacher an' all? Hmm. Has money to be always involved? Was the King's shillin' took by anyone? Aye an' maybe the most important question of them all: was there only one? Can anyone be a traitor for Good? Did ye ever think o' that? Think on that young man. Could bein' a traitor ever change things for the better, eh? Aye an' I'll say it again for ye to think on. Was there only the one?'

My mouth must have fallen open for his smile broadened as he looked at my astonishment with shrewd eyes that had seen a lifetime of history, treachery and change.

'If you can't work that out yourself, young fella,' he said softly, 'then you're not as clever as I take ye for an' shouldn't be attemptin' to write stories. All I'm sayin', me boy, is that, though he wasn't aware of it at the time, after the first half-dozen runs, the lad's last few trips had him in no danger at all, save o' course by accident wi' a trigger-happy Tan! Fish? Fertiliser? Rifles?'

'You mean?!' I stammered, completely at a loss.

He just looked at me steadily, the slow smile returning to the wrinkled, old face as he said, ''Tis a strange law that. Can't understand it yet.'

I looked puzzled at this change of subject but he went on, tapping out the pipe dross into the ashtray.

'Ye can't libel the dead but ye can get into all sorts of trouble if ye libel the livin'. Never understood that! Surely a man's name counts for somethin', dead or alive?'

Twenty-six

He turned to the girl behind the bar.

'Mary, are ye goin' to bring me a drink before I thirst to death?'

She looked across and shook her head at me.

'No more now,' she said. 'Come on, tea-time. I can smell Barry Ryan's sausages spittin' in the pan. Ups-a-daisy!'

She helped him from the chair and set his hat firmly on his still full head of grey hair.

'Off ye go now. See ye later when your mates come in for the cards. I'll rap the hatch,' and with a wave and a wink for me, he went gingerly down the steps to the street, leaning heavily on his stick. She watched till he was safely into the next house below, then came back, shutting the door behind her.

'A pint, John? On the house!' she asked, adding, 'He'll have a bit of lunch now and a wee sleep.'

'Thanks, Mary,' I answered, for we were long since on first name terms, and indeed a great deal more than that, for from the very first day I met her, I knew my life was changed.

She went round the end of the counter and reached for the tall black handle on the pump as I rose and went up to lean on the bar. 'You wouldn't take him for eighty-two, would ye? Eighty-three in November an' Granny's seventy-eight. Oh they're still able to get about a bit.

'They still take their annual holidays in the big Hotel on the cliff in Kilkee in County Clare. Always County Clare! Went first in the late thirties, I'm told, an' loved it so much they never go anywhere else. Goin' there for the past forty-five years or more in October when the season finishes. Oh long before even Mammy's time! Looked on as part of the furniture now I shouldn't wonder. There's a lovely, long, sandy beach there. D'ye know it at all? Easy walking. No hills. Still thinks he can't be done without, though.

'You're doin' him a pile o' good, ye know. Loves to talk about the good old days. Huh, from what I can hear, I call them the bad old days instead.'

She laughed showing those white even teeth and her green eyes, beneath the dark curls, sparkled into mine and there and then I knew I'd be coming back to Castletownshend, drawn not only by the allure of this friendly little West Cork village, nor indeed the beautiful scenery surrounding it.

'I run them into Skibb every Market day as well to make their ceilidhe with the few old friends still alive.'

She slid the creamy-topped pint across the bar and when her hand touched mine she let it linger momentarily and my idle thoughts about the future began to form into definite plans.

'They were left this place and ran it for years till well into the sixties, when Mum and Dad took over. They and I do all the work now of course. We love them dearly but ye still have to pretend to take orders from Granny Mary and Grandpa Brendon!'

Epilogue

It was a cold, starlit evening three days before Christmas. Unusually for that part of Ireland, rime bearded tree and bush across the river, with a fresh breeze rippling its dark water. I zipped my fleece to the collar as I stepped from the West Cork Hotel foyer and walked along its side wall to the car park. As I eased the old Morris Minor up the hill and turned left into Bridge Street, I couldn't help making the comparison with the scene I had described in my story. Hundreds of fairy lights hung from pole to pole, baubles and Christmas trees adorned every shop window, even Baby Hanna's normally no-nonsense Bar sported a coloured lantern hanging over the entrance. Rosy-faced adults and children, loaded down with purchases, jostled and bantered along the narrow pavements, spilling over into the street so that vehicles were forced to crawl at three miles an hour and virtually nudge some revellers out of their path with the bumpers. Skibbereen had left Mary's bad old days to the history books where they belonged.

I turned down Townshend Street, glancing at Dinny's public house, resplendent in coloured bulbs and cotton wool snow, inviting the world into its beer-barrel tables and bus-seated lounge, separated from the riff-raff of the public bar by an orange box nailed to the counter. I smiled at the memory of Mary and I sitting close there at Halloween, regaled by the old blacksmith's yarns, lies and legends, thinking that Somerville and Ross hadn't too far to go to find their subject matter for their *Tales of an Irish R.M.*

I left the busy town with its bulging streets and headed down the less than pristine road towards the sea and my destination. My heart began to beat faster as I topped the ridge and began the winding descent into the village. I had telephoned from the Hotel when I checked in and now I could hardly wait to see her and tell her my news. She must have been watching from the window for the car had barely stopped on the high-cambered street when the pub door flew open and the smile and embrace that greeted me completely dissolved any lingering doubts I might have had over my monumental decision.

'Oh John, John,' she cried, ''tis Santa Claus himself, ye are. Come away in till I get a look at ye. Oh John.'

And to the hoots and cheers of her customers, she put her arms round my neck and kissed me right there in the middle of the floor, while her Grandfather raised his pint to me and cheered with the rest.

'Glad to see ye, lad. Maybe we'll get a bit o' service now. She's been in an' out of that damn door all evenin',' he said. 'A Merry Christmas. What'll ye have?'

'I could murder a pint, Mary,' I answered, turning to her and sitting down beside him in his private corner.

'Long auld journey,' he commented.

'Aye it is that,' I replied, 'but the ring road round Dublin and the toll bridge are a great help. The whole cut is three hundred and nineteen miles.'

'Boys but that's a fierce dander,' he said.

Mary set down my drink and flashed that smile at me before returning to her other customers. My whole being warmed and, checking the small ring box was safely in my pocket, I settled back on the cushioned bench, at peace with the world.

'What's it like up there now?' her grandfather asked. 'Still as bad?'

‘Aw there seems to be no end to it,’ I said wearily, for it wasn’t a subject I wanted to dwell on at all.

There was another long silence, then he said, not looking at me but down at his feet. ‘I don’t want ye to take offence lad but did you lean to one side or the other or were ye strictly a down-the-middle-man?’

Suddenly I felt the anger rising in me and my warm contentment instantly vanished. I was about to snap a reply but he saved me spoiling entirely our relationship. He had seen the reddening anger in my face and, raising a hand to forestall any reply, went on hastily, ‘No, no John. Don’t be offended. I’m not interested in the particular so long as my little Mary isn’t harmed.

‘I just want to make a point, just between ourselves. After all didn’t I tell you the whole piece down here for your book an my own part in it? Your answer’ll never pass these lips just like Michaeleen’s beyond in the new graveyard by the chapel.’

He paused to let his remark sink in, then, tapping his mouth, went on, ‘They’ll not be around for very much longer anyway. I made eighty-three there in November, ye know.’

I was silent, wondering why he was pursuing this line of inquiry, and my uncomfortable interview with my Headmaster forced itself back into my thoughts.

He had raised his eyebrows in astonishment, incongruously dark against his shining pate.

‘You’re leaving at Christmas? Why, man? Why? Haven’t you a good steady post here? Are ye out of your mind?’

I told him almost in one word – Mary – and he snorted down his aquiline nose over his thin Errol Flynn moustache.

'You're a fool, man. A damned fool. You think they want you down there? Anyway you haven't the Irish. It's compulsory you know and that is if they even recognise your qualifications. No sir, you'll not just walk into a job down there!'

I didn't answer, standing there and feeling like a naughty pupil, waiting for his punishment. He got up from behind the big desk and opened the door to look up and down the corridor, letting into the study the shrieks, shouts and laughter of some three hundred unruly charges. Then, closing it again deliberately behind him, he returned to his leather armchair, lifted a pen and started to tap the blotter pad in front of him.

'And what about your commitments up here?' he continued.

'You know well, Mr Gallagher, that I have no family left here. I'm on my own with none to answer for but myself. I—'

He cut me short with an angry wave of his hand, dismissing my remark as irrelevant.

'I don't mean that,' he snapped. 'What about the cause we're in the middle of? Huh! Did you think of that? Did that ever enter your plans?'

Indeed I had thought of it. For weeks I had thought of little else; of telephoning warnings with the code word; the back-room meetings in the pubs in the small hours; the trips all over the six counties delivering orders, dates and times and the rest, constantly running the gauntlet of RUC and Army patrols, standing against both sides, no matter what their detractors allege.

Oh yes, Master bloody Gallagher, I had thought of it and, prompted by my story, questioned its legitimacy or otherwise, against the majority wishes of the people. Nor, Master bloody dyed-in-the-wool Gallagher, with your blinkered certainties, could you know the indescribable relief, when, after meeting Mary and that beautiful month of summer swims and evening walks had made my decision for me, to quit, before I had actual blood on my hands. Now it was done and I was back to spend my life in Cork, three hundred miles and one lifetime away from it all, hoping fervently that, like Brendon, they would leave me alone.

'Ach, get out. No such thing as loyalty these days,' he growled as I closed the study door on him, his unswerving views, and a troubled chapter of my life.

Pushing those thoughts from my mind, I sipped my pint and thought deeply about his question and its implications, for I had my own ideas about the different characters in the story I had almost completed. As I laboured before the old typewriter in my two-roomed flat in University Avenue, I had become more and more familiar with those characters and their motives and loyalties and, allowing for my author's license here and there, I wasn't exactly sure that it was all the unvarnished, not to mention unbiased, truth. I don't know who said, 'When legend and life contradict, print the legend', but I suppose he had a point. After all, history has always been written by the victor.

I looked at my elderly companion steadily.

'Yes, I was involved,' I answered him guardedly and without any embellishment.

He nodded to himself with a little grin of satisfaction.

'An' now you've left it, your side, whatever side that was, to come down here to marry my lovely granddaughter,' he said thoughtfully.

It was a statement, not a question, but I answered,

'Yes, sir. I love her with all my heart and she loves me just as much.'

'Oh aye,' he said. 'I can see that. Just look at that face, glowin' with happiness. Oh I have no doubt about that but let me come to my point so that ye don't think I'm a feckin old busybody stickin' his nose in where it has no business.'

My anger had gone for there was none on his side and I turned to face him, beginning to realise that I was completely misunderstanding the whole situation.

'Well, go on. Make your point. I want there to be nothing between us that might cause her pain for you know she loves you dearly.'

He tasted his drink and, setting it down deliberately on our table, tilted his head like a wise old owl. Then, after one of his long, 'hen's teeth' pauses, he turned to stare at me, and that slow smile which I knew so well added creases to the weathered face as he spoke.

'You left whatever side ye were on an' that's your own business?'

I nodded.

'Well will ye answer me this? It's just a wee notion I've been ponderin' on, wi' a mind to all the stuff we talked about over the summer.

Have ye altered in any shape or form, yer definition of a traitor, or will ye just join the club and damn us all?'

I noted the word 'us' while we stared at each other steadily for long moments, revisiting the several characters and situations in my notebook before grins spread across our faces and turned to chuckles which broke into laughter, so that Mary looked over at us inquiringly.

'Your grandfather's wee private joke at my expense,' I said by way of explanation as she set down two steaming glasses of hot, cloved and lemoned whiskey saying, ''Tis just lovely to hear you both. Happy Christmas to my two best boys.'

And as she returned to her other customers in the crowded bar, we touched glasses and sipped, settling back into the cushioned comfort of the snug and the Seasonal Good Will.

We sat in contemplative silence, each lost in the past and as the roaring turf fire and the hot toddy lulled us into the Christmas bonhomie, I could hear my father rustling the newspaper by our kitchen range and remarking to my sister Betty after some mild controversy which she had settled with the dictionary, 'Och! Dictionaries be damned.' And you know, his son could not help but agree with him.

Acknowledgements

Barry and Detta Ryan of Skibbereen for their friendship and local knowledge.
Keith, my son, for his cover design and Keith Shackleton and Dr. Paul Vincent for their publication and editorial work.
My brother Mervyn for his taxiing me over all the sites mentioned and his challenge to write the book in the first place.
Clarke Small for his acquisition of the rail networks of the time.

And Dorothy, my wife, for just being Dot.

I also acknowledge Professor Peter Hart for his 'The IRA and Its Enemies', which I have taken the liberty of fictionalising for the purpose of dramatising the ambush at Kilmichael.

A. J. S. Crawford

24765679R00080

Made in the USA
Charleston, SC
06 December 2013